MW01065911

# The Story

# Of

# Esther

# The Story

# Of

# Esther

## My Book by Danielle James

© 1999, 2001 by Danielle James
All rights reserved. No part of this book may be reproduced,
stored in a retrieval system, or transmitted by any means,
electronic, mechanical, photocopying, recording, or otherwise,
without written permission from the author.

ISBN: 0-7596-1019-3

This book is printed on acid free paper.

1stBooks – rev. 10/08/01

# *Table of Contents*

*Chapter 1*      *The Teachings of Esther* .......................... *1*

*Chapter 2*      *The Feast* ........................................ *26*

*Chapter 3*      *Esther at the Palace* ........................ *37*

*Chapter 4*      *The Wedding* ................................... *50*

*Chapter 5*      *Esther as Queen* ............................. *62*

*Chapter 6*      *The Decree* ..................................... *75*

*Chapter 7*      *The Fall of Haman* ......................... *89*

*Chapter 8*      *The Plot* ........................................ *101*

*Chapter 9*      *The Executions* ............................. *116*

*Chapter 10*      *The Massacres* ............................. *148*

*Chapter 11*      *Attempted Murders* ...................... *169*

*Chapter 12*      *Peace in the Kingdom* ................. *185*

# Chapter 1

## The Teachings of Esther

*A long, long, time ago, in a majestic land of high plateaus, and green valleys contrasted with deserted stretches of white Persian sand trails in the province of Shushan, there lived a young girl named Esther.*

*As the bright sun shined on her silky black hair, through the open bedroom window, her petite body arose as she sat up in her bed. She heard a knock at her door. Rubbing the sleep from her eyes, she heard a familiar voice.*

*"It's time to get up, Esther."*

*"Yes, Uncle Mordecai. Right way."*

*Esther placed her dark brown burlap dress over her slender body. She walked from her bedroom to the kitchen window, only to notice Uncle Mordecai. His dark coarse hair was brushed evenly back behind his ears. The very ends of his hair lay upon his broad shoulders. Suddenly, a small breeze filled the air, his gray temples and sideburns lay flush against his face, as his tainted gray beard was blown against his masculine chest. Mordecai brushed their only horse. The muscles in his arms protruded through the white cotton cloth tunic that was lined with sweat from the many strokes he made upon their horse.*

*Esther called to him from the kitchen window.*

*"I'm starting breakfast, Uncle."*

*"Ok darling, just call me when breakfast is ready and I'll be right in after I finish brushing the horse down."*

*Esther began to perform her daily chores of sweeping the floor, dusting the rugs, and feeding the sheep, while she prepared breakfast.*

*The minutes passed quickly. Esther hurried to do her chores and complete breakfast.*

*"Uncle Mordecai, breakfast is ready and I have placed it on the table. Please come and eat while it is hot."*

1

*Mordecai let the horse graze about the yard. He washed his hands in a nearby pale of water that sat at the front door.*

*"You know, Esther you don't have to do all of the chores first thing in the morning."*

*"I know, Uncle, but I want to get my daily chores out of the way, so if I have other things I would like to do, my chores are all done."*

*"That's fine, Esther," smiled Uncle Mordecai, "Come and sit at the table. Rest yourself. You are sweating as much as I am. Let's have our breakfast. You may say grace this morning."*

*As they sat across from each other at the old wooden breakfast table, Esther bowed her head slowly.*

*"Dear God, we thank You for the food we are about to receive and waking us up this morning to start another day in Your honor, my Lord. May this day be a blessed day for all. Amen."*

*"Very nice," Mordecai stated as he bit a piece of fruit.*

*"Thank you, Uncle."*

*"Esther, I would like to ask you a question. Do you know what you want to do with your life?"*

*"No. But at fourteen, I haven't really thought that much about it, Uncle. But I do know that whatever I do, I am going to do God's will?"*

*"That's wonderful, Esther, I can see some of my teaching is rubbing off on you. You know, I don't know what your calling will be from the Lord. But, I do know it will be something great."*

*"Uncle Mordecai, may I speak freely?"*

*"Of course, Esther, you are like the daughter I never had. When your parents passed away, you were just six months old. Before you came into my life, I thought my life was complete. But, since I've raised you, I realize you were a missing part of my happiness. So don't let anything upset you and you not tell me. I want to help solve whatever is troubling you."*

"*Uncle, on the days I go to the well to replenish our supply of water, the other girls at the well make fun of my dress. I know this is not right Uncle. I have done nothing to make these girls dislike me. I even tried to speak to them just in conversation. But they ignore me. They all just ignore me, except for Porthea.*"

"*Porthea?*" *thought Mordecai.*

"*You know the girl that I invited over to our house? She ate dinner with us one night about two weeks ago.*"

"*Ohhhhh, yes. Porthea. She seemed to be a very nice girl. But, you're right my darling, it's not right that they make fun of you in any manner. But, you still must understand that everyone doesn't love the Lord the way you or I do. They do not live by His rules. We should always treat each other, as you would want to be treated. They shouldn't tease you Esther. But, even if they don't want to treat you right, we must try to always do what the Lord would want us to do. Do you understand?*"

"*Yes, Uncle. But, what am I to say or do when I go back to the well?*"

"*Say this, Esther, "I may not be dressed in clothes made of silk or shoes of the finest leather, but, I do thank God for what I do have.*"

"*Ohhhh, Uncle Mordecai, I know you are right, but it is so hard to do the right thing sometimes. And I am almost certain they will laugh at me when I tell them such words.*"

"*Let them laugh, for God will be the one who judges you, not them.*"

"*Yes, Uncle you're right. God is the only one I must satisfy. I will be on my best behavior, but it will be hard.*"

"*I can't ask for more than that. Esther, I just want you to understand, we thank God for the food we have on our table and the water we drink and the shelter over our heads. Without Him, we could have nothing.*"

"* I understand, Uncle, I understand.*"

"*Now let's finish our breakfast. I'm going to ride into town and see the King.*"

"*You're going to see King Ahasuerus?*" *Esther asked, surprisingly, "I thought you had to be summoned by the King in order to see him."*

"*Yesssss. That is true, Esther. I was summoned by the King.*"

"*But Uncle you are neither his staff nor a nobleman.*"

"*That's where you are wrong. You see, months ago I was standing in the town square. I overheard two of the King's guards speaking of treason. I couldn't believe what I was overhearing. I knew those two guards from the palace. I alerted the Chief of Security, who was Hazor, a real good friend of mine. Little did I know at the time that Hazor, Bigthana and Teresh, the two guards I saw at the square, were all in on a plot to overthrow the King.*"

"*Well, how did you alert the King?*" *asked Esther, intrigued by the story.*

"*Thinking that Hazor had everything under control, I went to see Hazor at the palace that day to find out what he had done about those two guards.*"

"*Why did Hazor let you come and go through the palace, Uncle?*"

"*I knew Hazor before he became Chief of Security for the palace. We were the best of friends. He and I use to herd sheep together until we grew older and went our separate ways. He had a thirst for power and I had a thirst for God. But being his friend, he told the guards that I could come and go from the palace whenever I wanted to.*"

"*Well, what happened when you went to the palace to talk to Hazor?*" *asked Esther.*

"*I couldn't find Hazor anywhere in the palace that day. But, as I was leaving the palace, I decided to check the guard's quarters one more time. That's when I overheard Bigthana and Teresh, the two guards from the town square getting ready to execute their plan. That's also when I heard Hazor's name mentioned as the head of the entire plot to execute the King.*"

*"What happened then?"* asked Esther, in eager anticipation of the events.

*"I hid behind one of the pillars in the palace as they came from the guard's quarters. I followed them to the King's throne room. The King was writing something. They watched the King for a few minutes and then made their move. They drew knives. The King heard a slight noise in the corridor. He turned and saw the two men. The King yelled for his guards, but none came."*

*"What did you do then, Uncle?"* asked Esther, anxiously.

*"I leaped from behind a pillar and jumped Bigthana. The King fought Teresh. We were both engaged in heated battles for our lives. I called out again for the guards. At that time, I guess Hazor must have thought I was one of his men. He came in with other guards, but to his surprise, the King was still alive. Hazor told the other guards to seize Bigthana and Teresh. The King and I had wrestled them to the floor."*

*"But, Uncle you knew Hazor was behind the plot, so what did you do then?"*

*"As the other guards seized the traitors off the floor, I informed the King that Hazor was behind the entire plot to take his life. At that moment, the King had Hazor and the two traitorous guards taken to the dungeon until their execution. The King thanked me and called me a nobleman. I left without giving the King my name. I felt so bad for Hazor. He chose to follow the wrong path and he paid with his life."*

*"Well, you did the right thing, Uncle."*

*"So, when the King called me a nobleman, I considered myself a noble man. Actually, any man that looks out for his fellow man before himself is considered a noble man in my eyes."*

*"But no one knew your name."*

*"I know, Esther. I didn't want them to know my name. After what happened with Hazor, I really didn't have any reason to come and go at the palace anymore."*

*"Didn't you realize Hazor's personality was changing?" asked Esther.*

*"No, I just stayed in touch with Hazor because we were such good friends. Sometimes he would even call me to the palace just so we could talk about God. But several months ago, before I learned of the plot on the King's life, on many different occasions, I would go to the palace to see him. Each visit I made to the palace, he had someone come and tell me he was too busy to see me. So I stopped going to the palace and he never requested my presence. I thought that maybe he was just too busy with his responsibilities to have time for me."*

*"Wow! Uncle Mordecai. So I guess Hazor's values were changing during those months."*

*"Unfortunately for the worse."*

*"So the King had to look for a new Chief of Security?" asked Esther.*

*"Yes. I heard a man called Haman was next in line or the most qualified."*

*"Since the King never knew who you were, that could be why the King is summoning you to the palace?" said Esther, guessing.*

*"Remember, I left before he knew who I was," said Mordecai.*

*"Maybe somehow he found out Uncle and now he would like to see you. Why didn't you tell me all of this when it happened months ago?"*

*"Esther, it was late when I got home. I didn't think that it was important enough to wake you from your sleep. Besides there was nothing you could have done."*

*"So you kept this tragedy to yourself," she sighed, "I love you Uncle and just as you want me to let you know when things bother me; I want to be there for you as well. Don't let anything hurt you and you not tell me."*

*Mordecai smiled. "Very well, you're right. I promise to share my pain and my joy with you too."*

,*Mordecai rose from the table and reached for Esther to give her a big hug. Esther looked up at Mordecai and smiled.*

*"Well, may I come into town with you?"*

*"Noooooo. Not this time. The King only allows in the palace those people he requests to see. But, I will be back soon. Perhaps another time."*

*Esther nodded her head and smiled. Mordecai exited the front door.*

*Mordecai rode his horse down the sandy white trails of Shushan, with tall, green leaf trees lined on both sides of the trail. When Mordecai reached town, he rode passed huge temples made of stone and marble. The marketplaces were filled with merchants selling clothes and food. Mordecai knew he was only a few miles from the palace gates. He galloped faster. The dust flew behind Mordecai. The image of the palace grew larger. He slowed his horse to a trot. He soon reached the palace gates.*

*"Open the gates!" shouted Mordecai to the guards standing at the top of the palace wall. The palace gates stood enormously high and made of solid steel.*

*"Who might you be that you wish to come through the palace gates?" asked Haman.*

*"I am Mordecai! The King has summoned me. May I enter?"*

*"Ahhhh, yes, Mordecai," the man answered flatly, "I am Haman, Chief of Security. The King is expecting you."*

*Mordecai motioned his horse forward toward the gates, but the locked gates did not open.*

*Mordecai looked up toward Haman. "Haman, I thought you were going to open the gates. You know the King is expecting me," said Mordecai, curiously.*

*"Before you come through those gates, you must get off your horse and kneel before me," demanded Haman, as he stood pointing down at Mordecai from atop of the palace walls.*

*"Kneel before you, Haman. Why should I do that?" stated Mordecai baffled at the question.*

7

*"It is the King's order that all men kneel before me,"* insisted Haman.

*"Haman, I kneel down before no man. The King has summoned me. May I come through the gates?"* Haman grew angry. *A deep resentment suddenly filled Haman's heart.*

*"Who do you think you are? You kneel down before no man!"* Haman echoed bitterly, *"By the King's order, you shall kneel down to me, now!"* He raced down the palace walls, his chest of armor clanging and his bulky hand fixed ready to draw his sword. His dark brown hair flapped behind his ears as he dashed toward Mordecai ready to fight.

*"Open the gates!"* Haman ordered.

*The gates opened, Haman drew his twenty-inch blade from his sheath and pointed it at Mordecai. Haman thought a show of force would strike fear in Mordecai's heart and bring him to his knees.*

*"Climb down off that horse and show me what kind of man you are!"* shouted Haman.

*Mordecai slowly dismounted his horse to face Haman. The confrontation was intense, as both muscular men stood locked eye to eye. Haman stared at Mordecai with an anger that bordered madness.*

*"Haman, as you can see I am unarmed."* Mordecai calmly explained with both hands open, *"I do not wish to fight you. A man of your fitness and superior military skills would surely surpass my own. It's just that, I'm a Jew and in my beliefs, I kneel only to my Lord and Savior God Almighty. I mean you no disrespect. If there might be something else I may do for you?"* stated Mordecai in a mild tone of voice.

*Haman's grand theatrics had not phased Mordecai in the least. Mordecai was very calm. He looked at Haman with no expression on his face. This arrogance for authority infuriated Haman even more. Haman became enraged with hatred for Mordecai.*

*"You no good Jew. You think you are superior to everyone. Don't you? You are the only Jew in this entire province that has*

*refused to kneel before me. But that's ok for now, Mordecai. I will not stain my sword with your blood on our first meeting."* *Haman placed his sword back into his sheath. He had no intentions of killing Mordecai since the King wanted to see him.* *"You are not worthy of my blade. I will find another way to deal with you."*

*"Haman, listen..." Mordecai began.*

*"No! You listen, you good for nothing Jew," Haman interrupted, " You will regret this day, Mordecai. I promise. I will get you for disrespecting me."*

*"May I come through Haman? I really would like to see the King, he is waiting."*

*Haman turned his back to Mordecai and walked back through the palace gates. Mordecai mounted his horse and rode through behind Haman. Haman heard the sound of a horse trotting behind him. He turned and grabbed the reins of Mordecai's horse.*

*"I did not authorize you to come through those gates, Mordecai!"*

*"No you didn't, the King did. Do you want the King to hear that you refused me, after the King, Himself, summoned me? Haman, I have business with the King. I only wish to find out why the King requested me to come. I mean no harm or disrespect to you," said Mordecai.*

*"Just because the King summoned you, does not give you liberties you can take freely." Haman still held on to his reins, "I am Chief of Palace Security and I say who comes and who goes!" Haman angrily stated. "I can make you wait all day if I wanted to. Then make up some story to tell the King as to why you were late. And if you tried to tell the King the truth, it would be the last story you tell! Do you understand me?"*

*"Haman, I know that you are Chief of Security and the safety of the King is your responsibility. But you have nothing to fear from me. I have nothing but great honor and respect for the King. Now may I please go to the palace?" asked Mordecai politely.*

*"Not unless you kneel to me first!"*

*"Then I will wait outside these walls until you change your mind," said Mordecai. He pulled on the reins and motioned his horse to go back outside the gates.*

*"Lock the gates!" shouted Haman to the guards. He looked at Mordecai, "You may as well get your sleeping clothes. I will not change my mind!"*

*Mordecai turned his horse to face the palace gates. He waited to enter. Haman stared at Mordecai through the steel barred gates as they were being locked.*

*"You'll regret this day, Jew! You kneel before no man. Ha!" shouted Haman. "This arrogance of yours will mean your death, I will break you down!" Mordecai spoke not one word. He sat high and stern on his horse with no emotional expression upon his face. He waited patiently. Not far from where they stood, in the palace study room, the King awaited Mordecai.*

*"Servant. Where is Haman? Send someone to bring Haman to me." The servant left the King's study room.*

*Moments later, Haman walked through the huge palace doors made of solid brown oak, to the King's study.*

*"King Ahasuerus, you summoned me?" asked Haman.*

*"Yes, Haman. What would you do for a man that the King wanted to honor?"*

*At that moment, Haman couldn't think of anyone but himself that the King would want to pay tribute to. He answered.*

*"Well, give him the King's clothing, the royal crown and the King's horse for a day and parade him among the town's people to be honored."*

*"Excellent idea, then hurry and bring Mordecai to me. He should be arriving soon. I want him to meet the Queen. Introduce yourself on the way here."*

*Haman couldn't believe his ears. In shock, but not alerting the King to his disgust, he bowed.*

*"At once my King." Haman turned and left to comply with the King's order.*

Haman strolled back to the palace gates. Mumbling unpleasant words, as he grew near to the gates. "Open the gates for Mordecai!" Haman shouted.

Mordecai heard the command. He met Haman when he rode beyond the gates. "You may have gotten what you wanted this time Jew, but, I promise you, your days are numbered. Now follow me!" Haman said angrily.

Mordecai followed Haman on horse back to the palace. Moments later they both arrived at the King's study room.

"King Ahasuerus and Queen Vhasti," said Mordecai. He bowed to the King and Queen. Haman did also.

"Ahhhh, Mordecai, come in, please," greeted the King, "I would like you to meet my wife, Queen Vashti." The Queen extended her hand. Mordecai placed a gentle kiss upon it.

"My husband tells me you are the man that saved his life." She observed his worn-out attire. She noticed he was not of royalty, a fact that quietly displeased her. "I would like to say thank you, Mordecai. If you will excuse me, I am sure you and my husband have much to talk about." Queen Vhasti looked to her husband. "I will see to dinner." The Queen bowed to the King. Mordecai and Haman bowed to the Queen as she exited the room.

"Have a seat, Mordecai." The King motioned to a soft plush couch in his study. Haman stood by the door and leaned against the wall with his arms crossed over his chest.

" Would you care for some wine Mordecai?" said the King as he stood and moved about the floor.

"No thank you, my King."

"How about you Haman?" asked the King.

"No thank you, Sire." Haman stood from the wall to give his response and leaned back again.

"Mordecai let me tell you why you are here. I was reading late one night in my journals. I found out you were the man who fought for my life months ago when two of the palace guards attacked me. I would like to repay you."

"What I did your Highness was out of great respect and honor for you, nothing more," said Mordecai.

Haman felt Mordecai was trying to deceive the King by being humble.

"Come, Mordecai," the King stated firmly, "Now tell me what it is you desire, cattle, sheep, more land, name it and its yours?"

"Nothing my King," replied Mordecai.

"Come now, Mordecai, every man has something they desire."

"My desire is to only live in peace and honor my King." Haman knew Mordecai was being gracious only to gain the King's trust. Mordecai may not have wanted anything right now, but later, when the time was right. "I can respect that. But, I feel as if I must give you something for your heroics. How would you like to serve as the King's Advisor to the military?"

Haman was in awe. Angered by the King's words he lowered his arms and stepped away from the wall. "My King..." Haman spoke aggressively. Not facing Haman, but still focused on Mordecai, the King raised his right hand. A motion for silence.

"You mean fight in battle?" Mordecai asked in disbelief.

"Noooo, Mordecai," the King laughed, "I have no doubt of your ability to defend yourself in battle, as you fought for my life months ago. But you are almost fifty years of age, your stamina in the heat of battle would be of great concern to me. I would hate to lose a man of your ability and wisdom, to the bloodshed of war. Noooo, not fight, but teach my men on the strategies of military combat."

"No thank you, my King."

"Would you at least consider it for me?"

"For you, my King, I will consider it," Mordecai reluctantly stated.

"But, I cannot let you leave without giving you something. Haman had an excellent idea!" said the King. Mordecai rose *from the couch.  Flashbacks of his heated encounter with Haman came across his mind.*

"What!  Haman?" *asked Mordecai, confused about Haman making a suggestion.*

"Don't look so surprised, Mordecai.  Haman why don't you tell Mordecai what you proposed."

*Haman approached the King.*

"No, you tell him, Sire.  I am sure he would be more honored hearing it from you."

"Quite right.  Mordecai you will wear some of my clothing, my crown, and ride my best horse through town for one day.  It will be stated in a decree tomorrow for the following day.  Haman will see to the arrangements."

"My King," *said Mordecai,* "I'm honored."

"That you shall be," *added the King.*

*Haman stood silent.  His anger mounted the more the King spoke.*

"My King.  Please.  I desire nothing from you.  It was my honor to prevent anything from happening to you."

"You are a true nobleman, Mordecai.  I respect what you are saying, however, at least let me do one thing for you."

"Yes, my King, but not parade around town and wear your clothes," *Mordecai stated graciously.*

"Then take one of my finest horses from the stables."  *The King turned to Haman,* "Haman see to it that Mordecai gets the horse he wants."  *The King looked back at Mordecai.*  "I will not take no for an answer."

"Yes, my King." *Mordecai bowed as he motioned to leave the room.  Haman was about to follow.*

"Oh yes, before you go, in a few months I am giving a seven day feast and I would like for you to attend.  It's in the honor of all my noblemen and I consider you a nobleman.  I will send you an invitation.  It's up to you if you want to come.  However, I would be honored if you would."

Haman almost choked. He covered his mouth with his fist and coughed twice. Haman had no expression upon his face. He was shocked.

"In your honor, my King, I thank you for the invitation," said Mordecai.

Mordecai bowed and started toward the palace doors. Haman bowed and followed after Mordecai. They walked down the corridor.

"You think you may have won this battle because the King has great respect for you. But let me assure you, I don't! Why didn't you tell the King of our encounter at the gate?" asked Haman.

"I don't need to whine to the King about my personal situations," stated Mordecai firmly.

"Why didn't you mention to the King about me not kneeling down before you, Haman?"

"The King doesn't need to know about my problems. You are nothing I can't handle Mordecai!" stated Haman boldly.

"Haman I don't want to battle with you. Fighting you wouldn't bring me any pleasure. There is nothing to be gained by hating you. Please, I would like to be your friend."

"Friend! Ha!. The only way you can be my friend is for your lips to kiss my feet! That's where I stand, Mordecai. Now, let's go to the stables and get your horse," stated Haman angrily.

It only took a few moments to reach the stables.

"Pick your horse!" shouted Haman. Mordecai picked a horse he thought Esther would like to ride.

"Thank you Haman. Until we meet again."

Mordecai mounted his new horse and pulled his old mare down the sandy white trail that lead from the palace to the outskirts of town. Mordecai galloped home. As time passed, he came upon the front door of his small rectangular clay home.

"Esther?" called Mordecai, uncertain of where she was.

"Yes, Uncle, I am here. I have just made some fresh bread, boiled some corn, and prepared some fresh fruits. Would you care for some?"

"No, not right now, Esther," Mordecai stated in a tired tone of voice, "Come, sit next to me. I want you to listen carefully to what I have to say."

"What is it Uncle? You sound deeply disturbed over something."

"There is a man named Haman."

"Yessss, Uncle I have heard of him. He is the top man of security at the palace. Is he not?"

"Yes, that's right. And right now I'm not one of his most favorite people."

"Why is that?" asked Esther.

Mordecai stood up from his chair and walked across the room. He turned back to Esther.

"Lord, forgive me. But Haman angers me. I will kneel before no man! Even though it is the King's command. This is Haman's desire that I kneel before him as if he were some kind of god." Mordecai looked to heavens. "Forgive me Lord, I know that I am to love my enemies." Mordecai glanced back at Esther.

"Uncle Mordecai, I know that God is our only true King, but if Haman can hurt you, why not obey King Ahasuerus's command?"

"My darling Esther, God is our King. I believe this strongly within my heart. If I kneel to Haman, I'm going against our beliefs."

"But all the other men do it, Uncle. They kneel before Haman."

"That's why he hates me so. I am the only male Jew that will not kneel before him. Esther sometimes it takes more courage to stand alone in your beliefs, than it does to go along with the crowd. I will not kneel to Haman or any other man, when I know God is my Father."

"What if Haman threatens your life, Uncle?"

"*Especially, then, Esther, I must be strong. I know that God will do what is right by me, when I stand in faith for Him.*"

"*Just be careful, Uncle, you know I love you and I would hate to see you hurt.*" *Mordecai smiled and reached for Esther. He embraced her firmly.*

"*Oh yes, my darling you were also right,*" *said Mordecai as he released her.*

"*About what?*" *Esther asked, curiously.*

"*Look out the window.*" *Mordecai motioned his hand toward the kitchen window. Esther looked and saw a strong, slick, black stallion standing at the front porch.*

"*He is a beautiful horse! Uncle.*" *Esther was excited.*

"*You were right, the King found out I was the one who saved his life and the horse is his way of saying thanks.*"

"*That's great! What else did he say?*" *asked Esther.*

"*Just that he wanted to give a small parade in my honor day after tomorrow. I would get to wear the King's clothes, the royal crown and ride the King's horse through town.*"

*A parade in your honor, that's wonderful Uncle Mordecai. All that as tokens of appreciation from the King. I think he likes you a little bit. Am I in the parade too?*"

"*No. There isn't going to be a parade. I turned the King's offer down.*"

"*Why, Uncle? You did a gracious thing for the King. You should be honored.*"

"*Thank you, Esther. But performing acts of kindness is something that should come from the heart; not because you think you should be rewarded for what you have done. Kindness and kind gestures should be a part of your natural character.*"

"*You're right, Uncle. I will remember that. May I ride your horse sometimes?*"

"*He is our horse Esther, although I did pick him with you in mind. What's mine is yours.*"

"*Thanks, Uncle.*"

"*You're welcome. Now let's get some sleep, tomorrow is a busy day,*" *said Mordecai, "Don't forget to say your prayers.*"

As the night fell and the stars settled in the sky, Esther and Mordecai rested peacefully that evening.

The next morning Esther had breakfast cooked before Mordecai awoke. The aroma of fresh bread filled the air. "Esther, you are up so early. Is there something going on today?"

"Yes, Uncle, remember I told you I like to get my daily chores out of the way?"

"Yessss."

"There is something special going on today. There is a man speaking down by the river. I heard he speaks glorious words of wisdom. May I go and listen to him?"

"Yes, since you have completed your daily chores. Pay close attention to what he is saying. I would also care to listen, but unfortunately, I can't go with you. I'm going to meet with some of our Jewish brothers today to warn them about Haman."

Mordecai placed his two strapped sandals on his feet for a short walk to a neighbor's house.

"So, just place a piece of fruit and two pieces of bread in some cloth and I will eat it as I walk to Brother Tabor's house."

"No, Uncle, you will not. That's not the way you raised me. Whatever you have to say to Brother Tabor can wait until after breakfast. You said that breakfast is a very important meal and no meal should be rushed."

"Of course, you're right. Please, fix me a plate."

Mordecai sat down to the table and awaited his plate. Esther placed the plate before him.

"Well, go ahead and eat Uncle."

"No, Esther, not before you join me. The whole point of eating together is that we are together, as a family. Even though I have things I need to do. I enjoy our time together." Esther fixed her plate and sat across the old wooden table with Mordecai.

"Give me your hands." Mordecai said grace. "Thank you Lord for the food we are about to eat and drink. Watch over us. Watch over your entire kingdom Lord, that we may do your will.

17

*Amen." Mordecai broke the hot loaf of bread Esther had just made and passed her a piece.*

*"Esther, I forgot to tell you one other thing that happened at the palace when I met with the King. He invited me to a feast in honor of his noblemen."*

*"That's wonderful Uncle, when is it?"*

*"I'm not really sure. He is sending me an invitation. So I'll show it to you then. But, I really don't want to go."*

*"Why not Uncle? You have never been to a feast at the palace before. It would be different."*

*"Yes, different. But not a good different. They will probably be smoking, drinking, dancing and other things that are not in line with our customs."*

*"Well, just pay your respects to the King and leave."*

*"That's exactly what I intend to do since the King said he would be honored if I came."*

*"Good, Uncle." Esther bit a piece of fruit.*

*"You know Esther I thought about what you said about the girls at the well. I want you to know anytime these girls bother you or anyone or anything bothers you, let me know. I want to know your problems as well as your joys. Don't try to handle your problems alone. It always helps to talk about them."*

*"Thank you, Uncle. I do feel like I can tell you everything. You remember the time when I was six years old, I fell and skinned my knee very badly."*

*"How could I forget," Mordecai smiled, "You turned your dress completely backward so I couldn't see the blood that had already bled from your knee onto your dress."*

*"I just didn't want you to see me in pain."*

*"I know Esther. But, it's not about holding pain all to yourself. It's about sharing pain with those you love. Because those who love you aren't there just for the good times, they are there for the bad times too. Your loved ones are your support. When you are down, I give you encouragement to stand back up and when you are up, I give you that support to stay up."*

*"We had this conversation once before, Uncle,"* Esther smiled.

*"I know. I just don't want you to forget,"* Mordecai smiled.

*"You know Esther you can really tell your friends by their support of you in the time of a crisis. If they are with you through the bad times, you have a friend for life. Anyone can stand with you when the days are good."*

*"I guess good friends are really hard to find."*

*"Yesss, Esther, sometimes they are. That's why you should choose them carefully."*

As fresh fruit and hot bread were eaten, Mordecai and Esther finished breakfast.

*"Thank you, my darling niece for a lovely breakfast and pleasant conversation. I'm going now, I'll see you later."*

*"Ok Uncle. I'm going to the river to listen to the man speak and then I'll come back by the well and bring some fresh water home. I'll just take the buckets with me."*

*"Why don't you ride the new horse?"*

*"It's such a lovely day. I want to enjoy it. I'll walk. Thanks Uncle."*

*"All right, Esther. I'll see you soon. I love you."* Mordecai walked out the door.

*"Love you too, Uncle."*

Esther cleaned the kitchen from breakfast. She grabbed two empty buckets that set by the door and walked toward the river. When she approached the river that seemed only a few minutes from home, Esther saw hundreds of people had gathered to listen. She found a spot on the riverbank and awaited the words of this man of God.

Meanwhile, Mordecai had reached Brother Tabor's house. He knocked.

*"Mordecai, to what do I owe the pleasure of your presence?"* smiled Tabor.

*"I'm sorry to drop in unexpectedly like this, but I just wanted to alert you about Haman."*

19

"The Chief of Security at the palace? What happened?" Tabor asked curiously.

"I refused to kneel before him when I went to see the King and he drew his sword upon me. I just wanted to let you know in case there might be some added pressure from the guards of the palace against the Jews."

"Mordecai. It's the King's order. Are you trying to get yourself killed? I don't know of any Jewish male that hasn't kneeled to Haman. But, I will spread the word."

"Just alert everybody to be careful," said Mordecai.

"Of course I will, my friend. You be careful."

Mordecai turned to walk away.

"I'm going to stop at Brother Esam's house on my way back home and let his family know. So I'll see you later. Thanks brother, take care."

Mordecai strolled down a path of green grass and white and yellow daisies until he finally reached brother Esam's house. During his walk, he noticed boxes and crates being carried by horses and carts to the palace. Just as Mordecai was on his way home, Esther had just heard the last words spoken from the man at the river. She was now on her last chore for the day, to fill the buckets with fresh water to drink. Moments later, Esther approached the well.

"Esther!" called a girl already at the well, the same age as Esther.

Esther glanced toward the girl, as she grew closer to the well, it was Porthea, her friend and the other girls who always harassed her. Esther smiled.

"Porthea!" said Esther excited to see her, "How are all of you? It's good to see you. All of you." Esther was trying to be polite to all the girls. Esther went to place a bucket in the well.

"Be careful, don't look into the well first, as ugly as you look, you may scare the water back into the ground," spoke Porthea.

The other girls laughed. Esther was stunned at Porthea for making such a comment.

"*Porthea are you on the side of these girls that harass me all the time? And why do you speak such harsh words to me? I thought we were friends. I invited you to my house, you broke bread with my Uncle and I, you ate our food, you drank our water, and now you treat me like this?*" asked Esther.

"*No, they are on my side. I'm the leader of this little group and they do what I say.*"

"*What!*" Esther was devastated.

"*You and your uncle think you are better than the rest of us. Yet you live in a one-room clay house, where the kitchen, bedroom and living room are one. Your clothes are rags, your hair smells of horse manure and sheep fur and your shoes are falling off your feet. Yet, you feel, act, and talk like you are royalty,*" stated Porthea angrily.

At that very moment, without warning, Porthea slapped Esther across the cheek. Then she pushed Esther to the ground. Esther, caught totally by surprised, dropped her buckets by the well only to brace herself as she fell backwards upon the hard dusty ground. Dust flew everywhere. The other girls watched in disbelief.

"*Why, Porthea?*" Esther sat on the ground holding her cheek. It throbbed from the blow she took.

"*My father says, you Jews are nothing but trouble makers. You go around worshipping some God that no one can see, instead of worshipping King Ahasuerus.*"

Esther rose to her feet, dusting herself off as she stood. Porthea jumped back beside the other girls. She thought Esther might want to retaliate.

"*You want to fight?*" asked Porthea in anger and more secure with the other girls beside her.

"*No, I don't,*" Esther spoke softly, "*If you didn't care for my company, why did you accept my invitation to come to my home?*"

"*The girls and I were just curious as to where and how you lived, so we could talk about you. I just pretended to be your friend. It had nothing to do with you being my friend.*" Porthea *turned from Esther to look at the girls beside her. "Right? Girls!"*

*"Right!" shouted the other girls in unison. They were afraid to disagree with Porthea for fear of being treated like Esther.*

*Esther paused where she stood. She took a good long look at these girls she was trying so hard to be friends with. Tears began to form in Esther's eyes. "You know, Porthea and the rest of you, my uncle has taught me to be thankful for the things I have and if I act that way, its because I am grateful for the things I do have. I could have nothing. My uncle has also taught me to respect those who speak ill of you, and love those who take advantage of you. I must say there was a time when I wanted to be like you girls, but I can see now that your beliefs are far different than mine. If you followed the path of God, then you would not have spoken to me in that manner. I am a child of God. But, I want to say to you now, even though you have hurt me, may God bless you all and keep you."*

*"We don't believe in your God, our King Ahasuerus is who we believe in. Right? Girls!" stated Porthea.*

*"Right!" Again the girls agreed with Porthea.*

*Esther was heart broken and in disbelief of what has just taken place. But she just wanted to know why. Esther started to draw her water from the well when she looked at Porthea.*

*"Porthea, I only wanted to be your friend. I wanted to be friends with all of you. Does the way I dress stop me from listening to you when you want to share a problem with me? Does the place where I live stop me from holding you when we are sharing a joyous moment together? Does my being a Jew stop me from loving and caring for you because you are who you are? None of these things should count toward being a friend. Do you understand?" said Esther with watery eyes.*

*"We don't care for your silly words, Esther. Take your water and be gone from our sight," Porthea stated firmly.*

*"That's right, take your water and go!" shouted the girls, as they enforced Porthea's words.*

Esther knew there was nothing further to say. Esther took her buckets and drew her water from the well. Some of the girls had sad faces as they thought of what Esther had said. They knew Porthea was wrong, but not one of them was strong enough to tell her.

"Goodbye, have a very wonderful day, all of you," said Esther softly.

Esther carried the two buckets filled with water back home. Her arms trembled from the weight when she walked home from the well. But Esther felt no pain. She had done this many times before. The only pain she could feel was of her broken heart for Porthea.

"Good riddens!" said Porthea. She tossed her nose in the air and watched Esther walk away.

As Esther walked from the well, the tears began to flow from her eyes, that each step she took, the grass underneath her feet looked blurred. Minutes later, Esther walked through the front door with tears streaming down her cheeks. Mordecai greeted her at the door.

"What is this I see? Tears in my child's eyes and red cheeks. Who has done this to you? Who has upset you, Esther? Tell me my child," said Mordecai.

"It's the girls of the town, Uncle. Each time I go to the well, I receive harsh words of some kind from one of them and today it was Porthea, she was very cruel."

"I thought Porthea was a good friend of yours?"

"So did I, Uncle, so did I. After I heard the man speak by the river, he spoke words of wisdom, much like you do. I was feeling wonderful. I felt like, what a beautiful day it is. Then I met the girls at the well and they ruined my day." Tears flowed freely from Esther's eyes. "I guess I didn't chose my friends very carefully?"

"No Esther. Don't blame yourself. You had no way of knowing that Porthea was being deceitful. You reacted to her kindness the way anyone would have."

"*They hurt my feelings, Uncle. And Porthea slapped me.*" *Esther sniffled and cried.*

"*I know Esther. What did you say to the girls at the well?*" *asked Mordecai, gently wiping the tears from her cheeks with the thumbs of his hands.*

"*I told them, God bless them and have a nice day.*"

"*That's wonderful Esther. If you keep giving words of love and kindness, I promise the cruelty will soon end. For God will not let you suffer unfairness from people, when you treat them with generosity.*"

"*That's what the man at the river said too. I know Uncle, but it still hurts.*"

"*Just hold true to your faith in God Esther and He will prepare a table of blessings for you in the presence of those who hurt you.*"

"*You're right Uncle. Everyday is a joyous day in the blessings we have already received. That's what you always say.*"

"*Good, Esther. Just remember what I'm trying to teach you. I would never tell you anything that is going to hurt you. I only want what is best for you.*" *Mordecai embraced Esther and she laid her head upon his chest. The tears stopped flowing. Esther looked up at Mordecai.*

"*I thought you went to speak to Brother Tabor and others? Why are you back so soon?*"

"*I did. I spoke with Tabor and Esam. They will spread the word to the others.*"

*Just at that moment, they heard the sound of horses galloping toward the house. Esther and Mordecai looked from beyond the kitchen window. They saw two men in full body armor. Mordecai went out on the front porch to greet them.*

*The horses stopped in front of Mordecai.*

"*We are messengers of the palace,*" *said one man.* "*We have been instructed by the King to bring you this invitation to the palace feast.*"

24

One of the men leaned forward from his horse to hand Mordecai the invitation.

"Thank you," said Mordecai. The two messengers turned about and headed back toward the palace. Mordecai returned to the kitchen and Esther waited to find out what the two men wanted. "This is the invitation from the King that I told you about."

"May I read it?" asked Esther.

Mordecai handed Esther the scroll with the King's seal stamped at the bottom. Esther read slowly.

"It is in the honor of the King's princes, noblemen, and scribes that a seven day feast will begin on the fourteenth day of June, that the King's nobleman, Mordecai, attend the King's Royal Feast, signed by King Ahasuerus. This is wonderful Uncle. This is only a few months away."

"The King and Queen at this moment must be preparing for it as we speak. I saw the servants carrying crates of food and boxes of wine to the palace while I was visiting our Jewish brothers."

"They will have pheasant, turkey, and fruit of all kinds, it will be a feast of all feasts," Esther said with a smile. "I bet they'll wear the finest clothes, woven in silk and lace. The Queen will wear the sweetest of perfumes and her hair designed to the occasion. Oh, Uncle it sounds wonderful. In what capacity will you serve?"

"Serve? Serve?" Mordecai stated solemnly, "I am an honored noble man. I will sit at the table to be served. Just because I don't have a title of prince or king in front of my name and the wealth of the other people I will be in the company of, doesn't mean I'm going to serve them. Enough talk of the palace's festive occasion, we have things to do."

"Yes, Uncle I forgot. Forgive me." She reached her arms out to hug Mordecai.

"All is forgiven. No harm done." He embraced her firmly.

# **Chapter 2**

## *The Feast*

*The weeks and months went by quickly. The activities at the palace grew more festive by the day.*

*"Uncle, it's almost time for the seven day feast to begin."*

*"Yes, three more days and the King will have a grand feast."*

*"Are you going to buy some new clothing for the occasion?" asked Esther.*

*"Noooo, Esther, I will not. If I could afford new clothes, I would buy some for you. Money is something I do not have a lot of. The little money we do have goes toward the food we eat. You know that. I will clean up what I have and I will present myself as the noble man that I am."*

*"But Uncle, your clothes are soooo old, what will the King say?"*

*"Esther, the King is a kind man. He is not about what appears on the outside, but what kind of man you are on the inside," Mordecai stated firmly.*

*Esther said no more.*

*They went about the next couple of days just like any other day. They did not concern themselves with this special event upcoming. The days seemed to pass quickly. The third day soon arrived. Mordecai was dressed for the feast.*

*"A solid white Terri cloth tunic with jagged edges at the bottom, draped from your shoulder to your toes and a brown rope for a tie around your waist," said Esther.*

*"What is wrong with that? Oh, I know, I'm missing a brown cloth draped across my left shoulder for a touch of royalty. Right?"*

*"Ahhhhh, no Uncle, you are missing a bandana for your head," said Esther.*

"I'm not going to wear one. But, that's the spirit young lady. I'm not dirty and I don't smell bad," Mordecai stated with a smile and Esther smiled too.

"Go Uncle, have a wonderful time."

"Thank you, Esther, I'll try."

Mordecai embraced Esther and walked out the door where his horse awaited.

Mordecai rode briskly from the bright moon that lit the pathway to the palace. He knew he would have to face Haman to enter. He soon approached the palace gates.

"Halt, you! Who goes there?" said Haman, standing from atop the palace walls.

"It is I, Mordecai, the King's most trusted nobleman."

"Ahhhhh, Mordecai, remember me?" Haman said sarcastically.

"Do you have the invitation from the palace that my messengers brought to you?" asked Haman, hoping that Mordecai had forgotten it.

"Of course." Mordecai held the paper before Haman, "May I pass through the gates, please?"

"You have not earned respect from me Mordecai. You wouldn't have that invitation if it was not for the King. If you want my respect and to come through these palace gates tonight, you will get off your horse and kneel down before me, now!" insisted Haman.

At that moment, Mordecai smiled and looked at Haman.

"You are a true nobleman, Haman. But that is all you are, a man." Mordecai spoke with a mellow voice.

"That's right, Mordecai. I am a man that wants you on your knees before me!"

"Haman, I respect you as a person and one of authority for the King. You have that right because of the position you hold, but God is first in my life and He will always be first."

"You traitor! Blasphemer!" shouted Haman, "What do you say about the King, then?"

"I give the King my utmost respect and honor, that a King deserves," said Mordecai.

27

Danielle James

At that moment, a countryman rode to the palace gates.

"Greetings noblemen, I am Prince Mbadja of Ethiopia, may I enter these gates?"

"Show your invitation!" shouted Haman.

The Prince took his invitation from his belt and presented it to Haman.

"You may enter Prince Mbadja of Ethiopia." Haman then turned to the guards, "Open the gates!"

As the gates opened, the prince rode through. Mordecai immediately followed behind the prince through the gates. Mordecai was tired of Haman's harassment when he knew he had the King's sealed invitation in his hand.

Haman turned and shouted to Mordecai as he rode his horse to the palace.

"We are not finished Mordecai!" shouted Haman.

Moments later, Mordecai entered the palace. His eyes were astonished by the vibrant kaleidoscope of colors that filled the corridor with red, green, orange, blue, and pink colors on the walls, the curtains and the paintings. The King and Queen had added new dimensions just for this festival since his days of Hazor. The pillars extended from the ground high into the ceiling, almost touching the sky. They were made of solid marble with grayish brown streaks of granite embedded in the stone, huge in diameter.

Mordecai walked down the corridor and he could here the soft music of harps playing in a distance. As he walked closer to the ballroom, he saw the assembly line of Kings, Queens, and noblemen waiting to greet King Ahasuerus and Queen Vhasti. Mordecai waited his turn. He was the last in line. When he approached them, Queen Vhasti observed him from head to toe.

"Mordecai, come." The King placed his arms around Mordecai's shoulders.

"You have met Queen Vhasti, have you not?" asked the King.

"Yes, my Queen," replied Mordecai. Mordecai reached for the Queen's hand. He laid a soft kiss on top of her smooth skin.

28

"*My Queen, you look radiant in your gown of lavender. The pink trim at the bottom of your dress clings beautifully with the shawl about your neck.*"

"*Yes, my dear, Mordecai is right. The dress brings out your slender figure and the jewels about your neck also accent your gown. You do look very lovely this evening.*"

"*Why thank you Mordecai and my darling husband. And, do I remember, Mordecai? Yes, my darling husband, how could I forget. Mordecai! Mordecai, is the nobleman that saved your life and I am most grateful.*" *The Queen looked at Mordecai's clothes. This poor rag wearing person. She thought his clothes looked ready for herding sheep.*

*The King reached for Mordecai's arm. The King was slender in build. His red lace tunic, draped from his shoulders to his ankles, brought out the colors of the gems in his crown of diamonds, rubies, and sapphires. The white sash around his waist clashed with the five jade rings he wore upon his hands.*

"*Look toward the ballroom, Mordecai, we have a smorgasbord of delights...leg of lamb, turkey, swine, fruit of all kinds, melons, grapes, apples and not to mention the finest of wines. Go in the ballroom and delight yourself. Please Vhasti escort him to the ballroom,*" *asked the King,* "*I'll wait here for a few more moments to see if any others arrive.*"

*Mordecai said nothing. He raised his arm that the Queen might place her hand upon it and they walked to the ballroom. Reluctantly, the Queen placed her hand upon his.* "*What's going on, Mordecai?*" *asked the Queen harshly.*

"*Excuse me, my Queen?*" *Mordecai paused, baffled at the question.* "*Nothing my Queen. I only wish my daughter, Esther, could see, what I see now.*"

"*Come now Mordecai, is your family of royal blood,*" *said Queen Vashti.*

"*No, my Queen,*" *answered Mordecai. They soon reached the ballroom, Mordecai dropped his arm and the Queen moved away from him.*

"*Then how do you think such a thing would be possible?*"

"*My Queen, I was only...*" *Before he could complete his sentence.*

"*Mordecai!*" *The Queen said harshly, "How do you think you are even here? Look at how you are dressed. Noblemen with riches do not dress and carry themselves as you do. If it were not for the fact that you saved my husband's life, you would not be here. You are not of royalty. There is nothing you or your daughter, Esta, did you say, could do for the King or I. You should be grateful we let you stand in our presence. Just look at your clothes, they are pathetic. You can't even dress properly to come to a royal ball. I only tolerate you because my husband does. But if it were left to me, I would have given you gold coins for your trouble and you would have never been permitted in the palace again. Do you understand me, Mordecai?*"

"*Perfectly, my Queen. I am but a servant to you and the King. Your happiness and his means a great deal to me. I have nothing but honor and respect for both of you.*"

"*Enough words! Mordecai. Eat what you will and be thankful you are in my presence,*" *scolded Queen Vashti.*

"*I am thankful, my Queen,*" *Mordecai spoke humbly. Mordecai bowed to her. The Queen turned from him.*

"*I am going to join my husband in greeting the noble guest. Make yourself at leisure Mordecai,*" *said Queen Vashti as she continued to walk out of the ballroom.*

*Mordecai turned to walk down the palace corridor behind the Queen. Insulted, Mordecai started to leave, but he heard the King calling him.*

"*Mordecai!*" *beckoned the King. "Why are you leaving? The festive events haven't even begun. Stay, enjoy yourself, please. I would be honored. Sit at my table. It's the one with the plush pillows of assorted colors and the finest of wines laid from one end of the table to the other.*"

*Mordecai nodded, yes, with an unwilling expression upon his face.*

"*Good,*" *said the King, he patted Mordecai on the back and gently pushed him toward the palace ballroom.*

The King and Queen continued to greet the noblemen and their wives as they came through the huge marble doors. After they all had entered into the ballroom, they sat at their respective tables.

"Welcome all!" proclaimed the King, "Eat, drink and enjoy, for the next six nights we will be in merriment because of our prosperous Kingdom."

"My King," said Queen Vashti, "I will take the wives and we will adjourn to the stateroom, as you and your noblemen have much to talk about."

"Yes, my Queen, the servants have prepared the stateroom well. Enjoy Vashti, as I know you and the wives have much to talk about too," stated the King, joyfully.

The Queen departed the ballroom with the wives of the noblemen.

"Come Noblemen of my Kingdom, fill your bellies full of food and drink, until you hunger and thirst no more," said the King with a smile.

Mordecai drank nothing and ate very little. The evening of the first day passed slowly. Mordecai grew weary of the festive events. He approached the King as he laid back on plush huge colorful pillows, devouring a leg of lamb in one hand and sipping wine in the other.

"My King, I am honored that you invited me, however, I cannot stay."

"Mordecai the festivities have barely began, you can't leave now."

"Sire, I have a young daughter that I must attend to. To leave her for seven days and nights without any supervision would be against my better judgment."

"I understand, Mordecai." The King took a sip of wine while he watched the court jester juggle balls. "Thank you for coming. Ride safely home, we will speak another time." The King raised his goblet. Mordecai bowed to the King and exited the ballroom. The festivities continued from one night, into the next, and then the next, until the sixth day and night were gone.

On the seventh day at the midnight hour, the wives in the stateroom had talked for days until finally they had very little to say.

"Queen Vashti," sighed one of the wives, "I have grown weary of all the events for this day. I wish to retire to my chambers for the rest of this night. Only if the Queen permits?"

"It does not meet with my approval!" angrily stated the Queen, "We'll retire to our respective rooms when I say so, understood?"

"Yes, my Queen," stated all the wives in unison.

While Queen Vashti was tired as the rest of the women, she wanted them to know who was in charge, even if it meant keeping them up well into the night. However, as time passed, she too grew wearier of the evening.

"Let's all retire to our rooms for the night. I have had enough food and events for the day," said the Queen.

All the wives stood. The Queen departed the room first. After she left, each of the wives looked at each other, shaking their heads in frustration.

The wives followed her, one of them whispered to the other. "We could have done this minutes ago," sighed one wife. All the wives went to their rooms, when they passed the ballroom, they could here the men laugh and the music play. The King and noblemen were still in merriment well into the early hours of the morning.

"King Ahasuerus," stated a nobleman. "I have a very beautiful wife that I have not seen in six days. Sire, I wish to be by her side at least for this one night."

"Great idea noblemen, Prince Alijahem." The King took another sip of wine, " We shall invite all the wives to come and join us this last night. But, I believe my wife is more beautiful than any of yours. You men judge for yourselves, as my wife enters the ballroom. Servant!"

"Yes, my King," answered the servant on his knees before the King.

"*Have the wives come and join us, but, call upon my wife to enter last, that all the noblemen may gaze upon her beauty as she walks into the ballroom. Understood?*"

"*Yes, your Highness. But, the wives retired to their chambers hours ago.*"

"*Then wake them, servant! Now go!*" shouted the King. The servant exited the room quickly.

"*Let's have a toast to our wives.*" Boldly proclaimed the King. He raised his goblet high in the air. All noblemen raised their wine goblets. "*To our wives, the most honorable, gracious, obedient and beautiful creatures that they are, may they always make men happy.*"

"*Here, Here!*" stated the noblemen in unison. The men continued to sip their wine, the servant woke all of the noblemen's wives first. Now he arrived at the Queen's chambers. The servant meekly knocked on her door as not to startle the Queen.

"*Who dare to knock at my door at this hour of the morning?*" said the Queen angrily.

"*My Queen, the King requests your presence in the ballroom at once. All the other wives are awake and await you there,*" called the servant.

"*Tell the King I am resting, the hour is late, and I will see him later in the day. Now Go! And do not disturb me again!*" yelled the Queen.

"*Yes, my Queen,*" said the servant.

He left her chambers and returned to the ballroom.

The King, the noblemen, and their wives awaited the Queen's presence. The servant walked through the door and kneeled at the King's feet.

"*What's wrong. She's not ill, is she? Why has she not come with you?*" asked the King, concerned.

"*The Queen is resting and does not wish to be disturbed. Not even by the King,*" said the servant, kneeling before the King.

*The King rose to his feet, outraged. The servant stepped back, frightened.*

*"What! What! How dare she not come when I call her!" shouted the King, enraged. His eyebrows were raised and veins became visible on his forehead.*

*The noblemen and their wives stood in amazement with their mouths opened and eyes widened. They stared at each other in disbelief.*

*"How dare she not come to me? How dare she deny her King?" Furious, the King paced the floor with clinched fists.*

*The King suddenly realized that all eyes were upon him. He calmed down and collected his thoughts.*

*"Listen all noblemen and wives! The feast is now over! You may return to your provinces, and I thank you for coming. Now go, please," stated the King, remorseful of the event that had just taken place.*

*"Yes, my King," shouted the noblemen and they immediately departed the ballroom.*

*Finally, after all the noblemen and their wives left the ballroom, two of the King's wisemen quickly approached him.*

*"My King," said Memucan, the King's most trusted wisemen, "You must not let the Queen get away with such disrespectful behavior. Let Queen Vashti finish her rest. Have two guards posted outside her door. Once she comes through those doors, have the guards take her to the edge of the city with her belongings and banish her from the land of Persia."*

*"But this is the first time that Vhasti has ever done anything like this. She is so beautiful and she does love me," said the King.*

*"My King, you rule over 127 provinces from India to Ethiopia. All the princes and their wives just witnessed an act against our law, by the Queen. You cannot let the other wives think they can be rebellious against their husbands and not be punished."*

*"But..." said the King.*

*"This must be done! My King,"* Memucan interrupted, *"What Queen Vashti has done is against our laws. There is no mercy, if you want to keep the respect a King deserves, especially from a King's wife."*

*"But, I still love her."*

*"The news of this act will spread all over the provinces before the end of the day. I will see the scribes now. A decree will go out today that Queen Vashti has been exiled from this Kingdom and never to set foot on palace grounds again. If she does, it will mean her death,"* said Memucan.

*Meres, also a wiseman of the King's staff, walked up to the King and whispered in his ear.*

*"I know this is a terrible time my King, but time heals all. This horrible day will soon pass and be forgotten."*

*The King lowered his head and waved his hand to Meres, a sign to leave the room. Days and weeks passed. The King grieved over the loss of his Queen. Finally, one day, one of the King's wisemen came to him just as a servant was bringing the King a goblet of wine.*

*"King Ahasuerus, you should not mourn over the loss of your Queen, as she did you an injustice, not only to you, but to the people as well,"* said the wiseman, Meres.

*"But I did love her. She was so beautiful,"* said the King.

*"Obviously, she did not respect you or the rules of the Kingdom and that is what matters, your Highness,"* said Meres.

*"Yes, you are right,"* the King stated, still obviously depressed.

*The servant listened to the sadness in the King's voice.*

*"Forgive me for interrupting, my King. If I may suggest, you could send out another decree, claiming that all eligible virgin maidens of every province will be brought to the palace and trained in mannerisms conducive to being the King's wife,"* said the servant.

*"She must act and conduct herself in this manner or lose her life. This will prevent any other incidents like the one with Queen Vhasti, from ever taking place again,"* said Meres.

"*I like that idea. Do you think I will find someone as beautiful as Vashti was?*" *the King stated, excited about the proposal.*

"*Your Highness, what really matters is if she can obey the King's command. Don't you think?*" *asked Meres.*

"*Of course. But she still has to be beautiful. Start writing the decree right now. I will sign it when you are finished. Don't delay!*"

"*It will be done today, your Highness,*" *said Meres. Meres walked quickly from the King's presence to tell the scribes to write the decree. The decree went out across the land that same day.*

## Chapter 3

## Esther at the Palace

*On this warm and sunny afternoon, Esther was returning from the well. "Uncle Mordecai!" Esther dropped her bucket at the front door and ran into the house.*

*"Have you heard?" she asked, barely catching her breath and sweat dripping from her face.*

*"Heard what my child?" asked Mordecai, reaching for a cool glass of water from the table.*

*"The word is spreading, that the King is looking for a wife."*

*"Yes, Esther, I thought he would be soon," Mordecai quietly replied. He took a sip of water. He pointed the glass toward Esther. "Would you care for some?"*

*"No thank you. Why didn't you tell me Uncle?"*

*Mordecai gently placed the glass back on the table. "Because I was hoping that it wouldn't come to this. I knew the King loved Queen Vashti as he always spoke of her beauty in my presence. I saw the decree that banished her from Persia. I felt it would not be long before the King would be looking for a new wife."*

*"I really don't have a choice about not going, do I Uncle? The decree states every eligible maiden," explained Esther.*

*"I know you must go Esther. I just wish you didn't have too, that's all," said Mordecai.*

*"I know, Uncle. I would like to stay here with you, but our loyalty is to our King."*

*"Well, we must pack your things and you may join the hundreds of other maidens that will be there," stated Mordecai with remorse.*

*"I guess so. You don't think they would miss me if I didn't go? Do you Uncle?"*

*"Esther that would not be the appropriate thing to do. I have great respect for the King and I know if you became his wife, he would love you as much as I do."*

*"Then I will be honored if you would take me to the palace Uncle," smiled Esther.*

*Esther gathered her clothes and belongings from her bedroom. Mordecai prepared their horses for travel. Esther rode the beautiful new stallion for the first time. Together they rode on their horses bare back to the palace. The trail seemed long to Mordecai that day. He knew he would miss Esther's companionship. They trotted slowly along the sandy path to the palace savoring their last few moments together.*

*"Uncle I have been thinking about all of those things the girls said to me at the well."*

*"For instance?" asked Mordecai.*

*"They spoke of my clothes, my hair, and my looks. And what if the King takes one look at me and sends me back?"*

*"Esther, beauty is in the eye of the one who beholds you. If the King does not see your beauty, don't worry, for someone else will. God gave you your features. There isn't anything on this earth that's not beautiful, because God created it to be so. You look at something and find it distasteful, while I may look at it and see the loveliest creature in the world. Do you understand?"*

*"I think so Uncle," replied Esther, a tone of uncertainty was in her voice.*

*"Well we are almost there," announced Mordecai, "Any other questions?"*

*"No, I just want you to know that I love you." Esther looked at her Uncle with tears in her eyes.*

*"Don't cry, Esther." Mordecai wiped the tears from her eyes. "God is watching over you and I will always be here for you too. Now, go. The palace servants will be taking care of all your clothes and things. Remember you will be trained before you are presented to the King. Trust in God, angel and everything will be all right."*

"*I do Uncle, I really, really do trust in God.*"

Mordecai and Esther stopped well short of the palace gates behind some huge trees. They dismounted to switch horses. Mordecai felt Haman would be standing on the palace gates and might see him with Esther. They embraced for a few moments. Esther knew it would be a long time before she would see her uncle again.

"We are here Esther, you must ride alone to the palace gates. I do not want Haman to see us together. Do not reveal our relationship or your heritage to anyone. Now go, they will let you enter. Just tell them why you are there. Remember, I love you."

Esther mounted their old horse and rode to the palace gates. Mordecai watched as Esther entered beyond the palace walls. Once the gates were locked and he knew Esther was safely in the palace, Mordecai, not using the concealment of the trees, climbed back on his horse. Unfortunately, Haman spotted him in the distance. "Mordecai!" yelled Haman, "Why are you here? Wishing you could come in and visit the King?" Mordecai rode closer to the palace gates.

"No," said Mordecai with a nonchalant response.

"Then, don't come here again unless you clear it through me!" Haman insisted.

"The King let's me come and go as I please," said Mordecai.

"I know and I'm saying no more. No, No, More! Not unless you get on your knees and kneel down before me! Understood?" shouted Haman.

"I kneel only to God Almighty. I shall not come again, unless I am summoned by the King," Mordecai spoke with a mellow voice.

"Then you will have a long wait. Be gone!" scolded Haman.

Mordecai turned his horse around and galloped down the dusty trail to his home. Haman quickly mounted his horse. He followed Mordecai to slay him. However, the faster he rode to catch Mordecai, the more Haman had second thoughts, knowing *that he was the King's most trusted friend. Haman turned his horse around and rode in the opposite direction, down the same rocky trail he rode every night, home. Soon he trotted to his front door.*

*Haman walked through the door. He saw his wife, Zeresh, sipping wine, sitting in the living room awaiting his return home. "Honey, I met that Jew, Mordecai, again today. He is the only Jew that refuses to kneel down before me, even though it's the King's command. He kneels only to his God, he says." Zeresh rose from the couch, placing her wine goblet on the solid gold table in front of her. She walked over to Haman and stared into his eyes.*

*"You are second in command my darling. It sounds like he is a threat to your position and authority. You must find a way to get rid of him."*

*"You're right, but how? The King appreciates Mordecai for saving his life at the palace."*

*"You are a resourceful man. Think! There must be some way of getting rid of him without the King's knowledge?"*

*Haman paced the floor. Zeresh could see the intense concentration on her husband's face. Zeresh left the room while Haman was in thought. He walked the floor for several minutes. Suddenly a thought crossed his mind.*

*"Zeresh!" cried Haman. Zeresh came quickly from the kitchen.." I have a plan."*

*"What is it darling, tell me?" Zeresh asked excitedly.*

*"Not yet, I must think it through first, but, I will present my plan to the King at the appropriate moment. I will pick the right time over the course of the next few months. But for now let us rest this night."*

*Soon the sun drifted down behind the clouds, another dusk fell upon Shushan. Esther was adjusting to her first evening in the palace. Hegai, Chief of the Servants met with Esther and several other maidens that evening in the palace corridor. The women stood with one bag in their hands that held all their belongings. They all looked around the palace walls admiring the beauty and elegance of this enormous edifice. Hegai soon got their attention. "Ladies! You are here for one reason and one reason only. That's to be prepared to meet the King. He is in search of a new queen. While you are being trained you will not converse with any of the key staff and you will speak only when you are spoken to. For this evening you will be sleeping in one room together. Now that I have all of your names, I will assign two servants per woman. They will train you until it is your time to be presented to the King. They will call upon you tomorrow morning to start your training. They will be your eyes and ears about the palace. Anything you need or want you will ask them. The palace is off limits to you except for the kitchen and your assigned rooms. If you are caught without your servants on the palace grounds or any other rooms without permission, you will be immediately dismissed. Now follow me and I will show you where you will be sleeping for tonight," stated Hegai bluntly.*

*All the women carried their belongings and followed Hegai to this one room. It was a huge room with no furniture or chairs. Pallets were spread on a colorful marble floor around the room for the women to pick a pallet and rest there for the night.*

*Unable to sleep well, being in an unfamiliar environment with several other girls, Esther stayed awake all night until a new bright sunshiny morning was before her. With a stiff neck and aching back from laying on the floor with only a blanket to cover her, there came a knock at the door. There stood twenty servants, two per girl in the room. The servants knew which maiden they were to train over the next few months.*

*"Esther!" called one of the female servants.*

*"I'm here," said Esther. She weaved her way through the other girls.*

*"Come with us," said the servant. They took Esther to her own private room.*

*"This will be your room until it's time for you to be presented to the King."*

*Esther looked around this luxurious room. The bed was huge, laid with soft colorful embroided pillows. The canopy top was very high above the bed, draped with light pink linen curtains. The window had beautiful dark blue curtains pulled to the side so the sun could brighten the room. A plush velvet chair was near the door. A huge mirror sat upon the vanity table where perfumes and make-up were placed.*

*"This is my room?" asked Esther, surprised at the size and elegance of it.*

*"Yes," said the servant, "We are going to bathe you in the sweetest of oils and perfumes and then, we will style your hair. We will get rid of all your old clothes and you will wear the finest of gowns woven from silk. We will teach you all your mannerisms before you meet the King. You may ask us any questions you like about serving your King," said the servant assertively. "Do you have any questions?"*

*"Yesss. What shall I call you?" asked Esther with a smile.*

*The servants looked amazed at each other.*

*"Why the bewildered look on your faces? Is it because I asked your names?"*

*"We have trained many maidens before you and none have ever asked our names," said one servant.*

*"They trained under you for months and never knew your names?" said Esther, puzzled.*

*"They were so obsessed with being the next queen, they tried to tell us what they were going to do. But no matter, as you can see, the King has not found a bride yet."*

*"That was very inconsiderate of them. So, are you going to tell me your names?" asked Esther again.*

*"My name is Obtisse, Esther, and this is Ababa." Obtisse pointed to Ababa. Obtisse stood five feet-five inches in height. She was stocky with dark hair and dark brown eyes. Ababa was a little taller than Obtisse and thinner with red hair and dark brown eyes.*

*"Then, Obtisse and Ababa, I shall be most cooperative," said Esther politely. Each day for ten months, Esther went*

42

*through daily training with Obtisse and Ababa, on how to walk, talk, and obey the rules of the kingdom. They became the best of friends as Esther showed kindness and generosity in her words and actions toward Obtisse and Ababa. Esther slowly wore down Obtisse's stern emotional exterior.*

*While training continued, a new maiden was presented to the King every day until Esther's day finally arrived. Obtisse alerted Esther that her day had come. Her hands began to tremble. She took short breaths. Obtisse could see the apprehension in her face.*

*"Relax, Esther, the King is not an ogre," smiled Obtisse, "He treats all his servants with respect and any maiden that might become his wife would surely be treated with even greater respect. Now, let's see you in your gown."*

*"But what if I say the wrong words to make him angry? What if he takes one look at me and calls the guards to remove me? What if..." Esther asked anxiously.*

*Before Esther could finish another sentence. "Esther!" yelled Obtisse, "Calm down. Ababa and I have trained you well for ten months. Just remember everything we taught you."*

*"I don't know, I'm so nervous."*

*"Remember to speak only when spoken to and obey any command that he gives you. You will do fine," counseled Obtisse.*

*When Esther finished putting on her gown, Ababa appeared. " I have come to do your hair and place the makeup upon your face, Esther."*

*"Please do, Ababa." Esther was seated. Hours later, after her hair, nails and gown were completed. The servants stood back and admired the results of their labors.*

*"My Queen, you are truly beautiful," said Ababa in awe, "The rose lipstick matches the roses in your silky black hair, the satin pink gown lay evenly upon your body and your blue eyes bring out the color of the flowers in your dress."*

*Esther smiled at the servants.*

*"Please, may I be alone for a few moments? Ababa bowed as if she were Queen and left the room.*

*"It's almost time, my Queen," said Obtisse, jokingly.*

*"I know and thank you for your beautiful compliments and gestures, but the King has not seen me yet. So, may I please be alone and I promise to be only a few more minutes." Obtisse smiled and left the room at her request.*

*Esther raised her long gown to kneel beside her bed. She began to pray.*

*"My God in heaven, my desire is to do Your will. I want to help others and be a messenger of good deeds. If this is Your will, that I become Queen, please give me the wisdom and courage to face the responsibilities that may come my way. In God's name I pray. Amen."*

*Esther felt a sudden calm come over her. She was not afraid any more. She rose to her feet. At that moment, she heard a knock on the door.*

*"It is time," said Obtisse, calmly.*

*"Yes, I'm ready now," Esther replied with confidence. The King sat in the palace throne room awaiting the next maiden. Esther walked down a long corridor, the King could see her from a distance. Esther grew closer. She walked with grace and elegance. The King's eyes widened. He placed both hands on the armrests. He rose from his chair.*

*"Stop!" the King shouted to Esther. Esther paused where she stood.*

*"Servants!" the King yelled, staring at Esther the whole time. Esther's heart sank. Her eyes closed and she bowed her head. She knew the King was dismissing her.*

*"Yes, your Highness," said a servant, entering the room.*

*"Bring me no more maidens," the King commanded. He still gazed at Esther. " I have found my Queen!" He boldly proclaimed.*

*"Raise your head my bride, that I may gaze upon your beauty once again. What is your name?"*

Esther smiled. She raised her head obeying the King's command. She felt relief in the King's presence as his kindness disrupted her fear.

The servant smiled too. He quickly departed the room to spread the news.

"My name is Esther, my King." The King reached for her.

"Take my hand. You are very beautiful. I thought I would never see such beauty again. Not since Vashti. You please me Esther. Come and sit with me on the throne."

Esther placed her hand on top of his and they both walked to the royal chairs.

"Please sit and listen to me carefully. I know you have been trained on what to say and do before me. But there is one thing I will not tolerate and that is disobedience!" the King said harshly. The King released her hand. He spoke bluntly. "Disobedience will bring you death!"

"I understand my King," Esther said softly, gazing into his eyes.

The King calmed down from the gentleness of her voice and the calmness in her eyes. His heart softened. He reached for Esther's hand again.

"Yes, Esther, I can feel that we will rule this Kingdom together."

"Yes, my King." Esther smiled at the King while he held her hand.

"Esther we will be married in two weeks and I will send a decree throughout the land today that all will know you are my bride to be. Tomorrow I will also introduce you to your staff. You can tell them how you want our wedding planned."

"As you desire, my King."

"In the meantime, I will have the servants acquaint you with the palace rooms and the surroundings, so that you may move about freely. Oh yes, do not leave the palace without my permission and you cannot come to me in the throne room unless I call for you, understood!" said the King aggressively.

"Yes, your Highness."

"Servants!" called the King. Obtisse and Ababa entered. "Show Esther, your new Queen, the palace rooms and grounds."

Obtisse and Ababa bowed to the King. They followed behind Esther from the throne room. When they were out of the King's sight, the servants jumped and clapped for joy. "We are so happy for you Esther," said the servants in unison.

"We knew you would win the King's heart. You have always been kind and considerate to all of us. Now you are Queen!" Obtisse said excitedly.

Esther walked with the servants down the corridors of the palace. She softly uttered a few words toward the heavens.

"Thank You, God."

While Esther was adjusting to her new position, Mordecai was tending to chores at home when he heard a knock at the door.

"Mordecai, Mordecai!" cried Tabor, one of the neighbors. Mordecai opened the door.

"Have you heard?" asked Tabor.

"Heard what, my friend?" Mordecai replied dumbfounded.

"Esther will soon be our new Queen!" Mordecai stood startled at the news, but bursting with joy.

"Come to the town square and read the decree posted on the walls of the city about our new Queen," exclaimed Tabor. Mordecai ran for his horse. He streaked to town to read the news that had already spread about Esther. Perhaps he might get a chance to see her.

Esther, meanwhile, was still adjusting to palace life. She was getting to know the servants and they, in turn, were getting to know her.

"Esther," said Obtisse, "I know the cooks well. What shall I have the cooks serve you and the King for supper?"

"My goodness!" exclaimed Esther, "I guess that is one of my responsibilities now, isn't it? I've had my thoughts on the wedding the King wants me to oversee."

"Yes, your Highness."

*"I'm still in shock. It all has happened so fast, I need time to adjust."*

*"Yes, my Lady. But you really deserve to be Queen," said Ababa.*

*"Thank you, Ababa."*

*"Well, Obtisse, do me this honor. I want you to send word to my uncle to come to the palace to see me and share in my joy."*

*"At once, my Lady. And who might your uncle be?" asked Obtisse.*

*"Mordecai. He lives near the northern edge of the province."*

*"Yes, my Lady, at once," said Obtisse. She turned and exited the room.*

*"What does the King like to eat?" asked Esther.*

*"I don't know, my Lady, but we may go to the kitchen and ask the cooks. If you would, follow me," said Ababa.*

Obtisse hurried to deliver the message at Esther's request. She arrived at the palace gates only to overhear Haman with his voice raised in anger.

*"Mordecai! What are you doing here? You are never to enter these walls unless summoned by the King or have you come to kneel down before me? State your business!" demanded Haman.*

*"Please, Haman, not now. I wish to see the King," pleaded Mordecai.*

*"Oh, you do, do you? Well, not today! The King has selected a new queen and does not wish to be bothered by the likes of you! But, if you kneel to me, I might see what I could do," said Haman.*

*"Thank you, but, no thank you," answered Mordecai.*

Mordecai pulled his horse's reins and turned around to head home in a slow trot. Haman turned and headed back toward the palace. Obtisse waited until Haman was gone from sight.

Mordecai had only ridden a short distance before Obtisse called to him from behind the palace gates.

"Mordecai!" whispered Obtisse, just loud enough to be heard. "I have a message from our Queen to be." Mordecai dismounted his horse and ran back to the palace walls.

"What did she say?" asked Mordecai, eagerly.

"She desires your presence in the palace, when you can. She wants to share her joy with you."

Mordecai smiled at Obtisse. He paused, he glanced down, and he remembered what they had discussed about sharing their joy and pain. When he looked back at Obtisse the smile was gone.

"Tell her, Haman, Chief of the Palace Security, forbids my entrance beyond the palace walls. My presence in the palace can only mean her harm at this point. However, tell her I love her and I will be watching at the wedding. I will try to see her soon and share in her joy."

"Yes, Mordecai, I will tell her," said Obtisse.

Mordecai left from near the palace gates, while Obtisse headed back to the palace kitchen.

When Haman entered the palace, he saw Esther coming from the kitchen.

"My Lady," smiled Haman, "You must be proud to be selected by the King. If there is any way I can be of service to you, please let me know. I am Chief of the Guards for the palace. They call me Haman."

"Soooo, you, are Haman," said Esther, finally meeting her uncle's adversary.

"Yes, my Lady, you have heard of me."

"Yes, Haman I have."

"Good things, I trust. Again, my Lady if you wish anything of me, do let me know."

"That is most gracious of you. I will do just that. I will call if I need you."

"Very well, my Lady, then I shall be about my duties of securing the palace." Haman had just left the room when suddenly, Esther heard a voice calling her name.

"My lady! My lady!" cried Obtisse, racing down the corridor to reach Esther. She passed Haman.

"Slow down servant girl, before you hurt yourself," smiled Haman. Obtisse stopped. Bowed to Haman and continued to walk the rest of the way.

"Yes, Obtisse, what is it. Why are you back so soon?" asked Esther, curiously. Obtisse looked back to make sure Haman had walked down the corridor out of sight.

"My Lady your uncle was outside the palace walls." Obtisse spoke almost out of breath. "Haman has forbidden him to come in the palace. I briefly spoke to him through the palace gates. He wants you to know that he loves you and will try to see you soon."

"Then I will speak to Haman now, since he is so willing to be of service to me," said Esther softly.

"No! My Lady," cried Obtisse, "You are not Queen yet. You have no authority over Haman. To give him a command right now, he would have a choice to honor it or dishonor it, if it suits him. You must wait, wait until you are officially Queen and then, state your desires."

"Yes, you are right."

"Right now, my Lady, your main focus should be the King, his desires and the wedding," said Obtisse.

"Yes, of course," said Esther softly, "I was just concerned about my uncle. It's been ten months since we last spoke to each other. His words of wisdom mean a lot to me. I just want to share this joyous time with him."

"His time with you will come, my Lady. Now let us go finish touring the palace," said Obtisse.

Obtisse showed Esther every room and introduced her to every servant they met. They walked about the grounds and stables. Esther was so exhausted. By the time they finished touring the palace, all she wanted to do was rest.

"I'm tired Obtisse. I'm not hungry. No dinner for me thank you, I'm going straight to bed."

"Very well, my Lady, until tomorrow."

# Chapter 4

## The Wedding

The next day, the sun shined bright through Esther's window, a knock came at her door.

"Who is it?"

"My Lady, it's me, Obtisse. Your breakfast is prepared. So we must dress appropriately. The King awaits you in the throne room in a few minutes."

Esther opened the door. "Hurry! Obtisse, help me get dressed." Esther did not want to keep the King waiting for her.

"My Queen we have a little time. I had the cook prepare a small breakfast for you in the kitchen."

"Very well." Esther slowed her pace and Obtisse assisted her in getting prepared to meet the King. "You know, my Uncle Mordecai always insisted that I have a good breakfast to start my day."

Moments later, Esther was in the kitchen trying to eat something. She was a little nervous, but she was able to eat some fruit and drank some juice. After a healthy meal, she immediately went to meet the King in the throne room. When Esther came through the door, she bowed.

"Esther you are right on time. Please, come take your place beside me." Esther went to sit in the Queen's chair. The King reached for her hand to assist her to her seat. He placed a soft kiss upon her smooth skin while they waited.

"I have summoned my staff. They will be here momentarily. I trust you rested well?"

"Yes, Sire, I did. Everyone was very helpful in showing me around the palace. I met some of your staff yesterday."

"No, Esther, our staff. Please, all that you see before you, is yours. Anything that you desire shall be yours. If it's within my power to grant all your wishes and dreams, I shall do so."

*"Thank you, my King,"* Esther smiled. *She thought of how wonderful it would be to have her Uncle Mordecai at her side, but she remember what he had told her of concealing their relationship. "At this moment there is nothing."*

*The King looked down the corridor. He rose from his royal chair made of plush velvet.*

*"Ahhhh, Esther, here they come now."*

*Down the corridor came a long procession of well-dressed servants. They entered the throne room. They stood in a straight line in front of the throne. Once in position, they bowed to the King.*

*"Members of my royal staff, I have selected a new Queen." The King reached for Esther's hand again and slightly raised it for her to rise before the staff. "This is Esther, your new Queen."*

*The staff bowed as the King presented her. She in turn, bowed to the staff.*

*"Esther," said the King, "At my right is Meres, Head Wisemen, next Haman, Head of Security, Harbonah, Head of Kitchen Staff, Ischdi, Head of the Scribes and Hegai, Head of all Servants. These are your key personnel if you need anything done. You may call upon the staff to perform their specific duties for you at any time."*

*"Thank you, my King," said Esther. The King turned to his staff.*

*"Staff you will give Esther your full cooperation, starting now, as if she were officially Queen."*

*"Yes, my Lord," they all said in unison and bowed their heads.*

*"Now in two weeks, Esther and I will be married. She has a wedding to oversee, give her your full cooperation or you will answer to me. She will be calling on you as the wedding grows near. Thank you." The King turned from his staff to speak to Esther. "Esther, do you have anything you wish to say?"*

*"No, my King. Not at this moment."*

Danielle James

"You may go staff." The King motioned with his hand toward the door.

The staff bowed and departed the throne room.

"Esther you may go now. The staff will be very helpful in preparation of our wedding. I will not see you again until our wedding day."

"Very well, Sire." The King kissed her hand. Esther bowed and left the throne room: She went back to her bedroom, where Ababa and Obtisse awaited her return.

"Obtisse, what am I suppose to do? I know nothing about royal weddings."

"Ahhhh, my Lady, the King knows that. Do not worry yourself. The staff will do everything. The only things you really have to do are pick your wedding gown, select the food you want prepared for the feast after the wedding, and oversee the decorations."

"Where do I look for a dress?" asked Esther.

"I will take care of the dress," said Obtisse.

"I will take care of your make-up, hair and nails," stated Ababa.

"My Lady, as the decorations are put into place, you walk about and tell the decorator," Obtisse pranced around the room and waived her right hand elegantly from left to right, "No, I would like pink instead of blue," you know, that sort of thing. But, if everything is fine. Then say nothing," explained Obtisse.

"Is that all I have to do?" stated Esther in a doubtful tone.

"Yes it is my Lady. But don't forget to consult with the wisemen on when to walk down the aisle. Now, come with me and we will pick out a wedding dress. If you don't like the ones that are already prepared, the dress makers will design one to your taste."

"This is so overwhelming."

"You'll get use to it. I'll be here to support you every step of the way," smiled Obtisse.

"Me too, my Lady. You can count on me," said Ababa.

52

"We will first check with Harbonah about the food for the feast after the wedding," said Obtisse. Esther was in awe of all that she had to do. She followed and listened to Obtisse as she had for the past ten months. Esther knew she could count on her through the next two weeks.

Esther spoke with Harbonah about the food, the wisemen, on her protocol, and Hegai on the gowns to be worn by some of the servants.

"There is one more person I must speak with, Ischdi, the Head of the Scribes."

"Why? My Lady. The invitations are going to be sent out to every Prince in the King's Provinces. I'm sure the process is already being performed as we speak."

"I want an invitation to be sent to my Uncle Mordecai."

"Oh, my Lady, I do not think that is wise. Haman sends the messengers to deliver the invitations. He would think that suspicious of you to invite Mordecai." Esther sighed.

"Come, let's look at your dress, as all around us, your wedding is being prepared."

Esther and Obtisse went to look at the clothing room for the Queen. Once they arrived, Esther was amazed. "My goodness!" Esther was astonished at the amount of clothes she saw.

"Yes my Lady." Obtisse pointed to each section. "One section is for your everyday wear, this section is for your dinner wear, this section for your royal balls, this section for bedtime attire, and the one we are searching for, the wedding section. Look through them and take your pick or we can make one. Your choice." She started to glance through dresses she thought suitable for a wedding.

"Why a wedding section? A Queen would expect to be married only once," asked Esther.

"That is true my Lady. But you also attend weddings of other royal families." Obtisse was still browsing through the gowns unaware of Esther's physical expression. "What do you think of this dress?" Obtisse pulled one from rack. For a brief *moment, she didn't here a word from Esther. Obtisse turned from the lavish wardrobe of gowns, only to find Esther with a remorseful expression upon her face. "Why the frown, my Lady?" asked Obtisse.*

*"Even in all the splendor of beautiful gowns, an abundance of jewels, and riches beyond what anyone could imagine, the one thing I desire most, cannot be granted."*

*"What is that?" asked Obtisse, puzzled, because of the frown on Esther's face.*

*"My Uncle Mordecai can't share all of this with me."*

*"My Lady..." Obtisse was looking to console her.*

*Esther interrupted, "Obtisse you pick the dress. No matter what it is, I'm sure it will be stunningly beautiful. I'm going back to my room." Tears formed in her eyes.*

*"As you wish. I will be there soon."*

*Esther returned to her bedroom, while Obtisse stayed to find a wedding gown for her.*

*All around the palace, the wedding was in preparation. The King was in his study room deep in thought about Esther and his upcoming marriage. When he heard a knock upon his door.*

*"Come in," said the King.*

*"Ahhhh, Haman, excellent. I'm glad you came by to speak with me. I have some things I would like to discuss with you."*

*"Yes, your Majesty. That is why I came. I would like to know if you want any extra men posted for security either at your wedding or the procession through the town square?"*

*"No, everything as usual."*

*"Very well, your Highness." Haman bowed and started to leave the room.*

*"Wait, Haman."*

*Haman stopped and turned around.*

*"Yes your Majesty?"*

*"What do you think of Esther?"*

*"She is a beautiful woman, my King."*

"*Yes, yes, she is, but there is something more about her. She makes me feel wonderful just being next to her. Do you know what I mean?*"

"*I think so, your Majesty.*" *Haman was baffled at the question.*

*The King could see that Haman was not interested in the conversation.*

"*Also Haman, I was thinking of inviting Mordecai to the wedding.*"

"*What! He's not of royalty, your Majesty,*" *cried Haman. His neck stiffened at the mention of his name.*

"*I know, but he did save my life and I respect the man. I would just like to extend him an invitation.*"

"*You gave him a horse already. If you think that's not enough, send him a few gold coins, but don't invite him to your wedding.*"

"*Sorry, Haman, I've made my mind up. See to it that he receives an invitation,*" *the King stated aggressively.*

"*At once, my King,*" *reluctantly replied Haman. He bowed and left the room. On his way down the corridor, Haman knew he couldn't invite the man that he hated so much to the wedding. The King would never know if he doesn't get an invitation. Besides there would be thousands of people at the wedding, the King wouldn't think twice about Mordecai not being there once the wedding had begun. He was not going to send Mordecai an invitation. Haman began his rounds to prepare the palace for security and to ensure all the other invitations were sent by messengers. At that same moment, Obtisse was on her way to Esther's bedroom with the wedding dress she had selected.*

*With both arms wide apart holding the wedding dress, Obtisse slowly opened the bedroom door with her back as her hands were full. Esther was lying across the bed still sad, while Ababa was gathering make-up and perfumes to be ready for the wedding.*

"*My Lady, behold.*" *Obtisse raised her arms to show the gown. Esther rose from the bed. Obtisse laid the gown down.*

55

*"Obtisse how beautiful it is!" exclaimed Esther. "But I'm not really in the mood to try on a dress right now."*

*"My Queen to be, we have less than two weeks. Let's try it on to make sure it fits. We may have to make you another one if it's too tight," said Obtisse.*

*"Yes, that is a lovely dress," agreed Ababa, "I'll help you try it on."*

*Minutes later, Esther was completely dressed. The wedding gown extended from her shoulders to her toes. The veil and the gown were a ·creamy pearl white. The gown had mesh embroidered with flowers from neck to shoulders. The rest of the gown was satin with fringed lace, designed in a circular style intertwined at the seam of the dress and the ends of the long sleeves. The train of the dress, also a creamy white satin, which Obtisse had folded in order to carry it, was twenty feet in length. The veil of the gown extended from the top of her head to the seam of her gown. Esther gazed in the mirror. "Obtisse the gown fits perfectly. We'll use this one."*

*"My Lady, this gown will go splendid with a bouquet of amaranth flowers, complete with satin ribbons tied in bows to match your dress," explained Obtisse.*

*"My Lady," admired Ababa, "You do look beautiful. Would you like for me to do your hair and make-up now too?"*

*"No. Since you know what I am wearing just pick the appropriate matching colors and a nice hairstyle. I trust your judgment."*

*"Thank you my Lady. It will be done," said Ababa.*

*"I'm tired and wish to rest for the remainder of the day. Please see that I am not disturbed. Let's take the dress off and you may prepare it for the wedding day, Obtisse."*

*As the days passed and the wedding day drew near, Obtisse and Esther made their final rounds in preparation of the wedding. They checked the wedding hall decorations, the food for the feast after the wedding, the gowns for the servants in the wedding and the invitations. Everything was ready. Finally the wedding day arrived. The town's people filled the streets, each trying to get a glimpse of their new queen when the procession rode by.*

*The wedding hall was decorated beautifully. The altar had plush velvet carpet all overlain with white and red rose petals all around. The middle of the wedding hall had a path of red carpet lining the marble floor. White and red stemmed roses adorned each side. Red and white satin bows were hung across the ceiling. The back of the altar was filled with lavish wedding gifts of gold, silver, diamonds, and clothes of all colors and fabrics. Beautiful rugs, ivory trinkets, necklaces, bracelets and much more had been given by the guests. Everything was in place.*

*On this grand day, the wedding hall was filled with Kings from neighboring countries, princes, noblemen and their wives.*

*When Meres stood in the middle of the altar with a piece of paper in his hand, the King approached the altar. He was dressed with his royal crown of diamonds, rubies and sapphires on his head. The solid black satin tunic he wore had gold trim about the neck, bottom seams, and long sleeves. A golden sash was worn around the waist that accented the gold trims. He wore open toed sandals with leather straps that went across the top of his feet. The King stood beside Meres.*

*Hundreds of people stood to watch this royal wedding. They anxiously awaited the bride-to-be. Esther was very nervous. She waited for the music to start. That would be her cue to walk down the aisle.*

*"Are you ready my Lady?" asked Obtisse as she pulled and tugged at the veil to make sure everything was straight. The veil was not worn over the face, but laid backward from her head to the seams of her gown.*

*"I'm ready," said Esther. She took a deep breath. The harpist began to play a wedding tone. Esther slowly walked from behind the curtains, two servants trailed her holding the twenty-foot bridal train. The King turned to watch Esther come down the aisle. Hundreds stood and heads turned to watch Esther come down the aisle. Although nervous inside, Esther*

*held her head high and with grace and elegance she walked down the aisle to meet her future husband. Once she reached the King, her bridal train was released and the servants moved into the crowd. They were not to block the view of the guest.*

*Esther faced Meres and so did the King. Meres began to read, he looked at the crowd.*

*"Kings, Princes, noblemen, fellow countrymen and wives, we have gathered here today to unite King Ahasureus and Esther into matrimony. This is a ceremony of divine love to one another and should be given all the respect and honor that goes into a relationship." Meres looked at the King and Esther. "Will you both face each other and hold hands, please?"*

*They both did as Meres requested. They gazed into each other eyes.*

*"I will now read the love poem selected by the King," stated Meres. He began to read from the paper that he held.*

*"We are about to take a journey together. The journey will lead us down long roads and short roads, but as long as we have each other, no journey is too long or too short. It has been said that sincere love is hard to find, but if love is true, it will find you. Love makes your heart skip a beat, but since I have met you, my heart has been pounding with joy. The day I stop loving you is the day my heart beats no more. If you could give me the sun, the moon, and the stars, none would compare to the greatest gift of all, your love for me. As we go from day to day, we will meet with trials and tribulations, but just to see your smile will make that day worthwhile. Just to hold you in my arms will give me strength and support to carry on. How much do I love you? I love you more than gold, more than silver, more than anything, more than life itself. I give you my emotions, my heart and my love, now and forever." Meres looked to the crowd. "That concludes the reading of the poem."*

*Esther smiled with joy.*

*"You may place the ring upon her finger." Meres reached for the ring from a table by his side and handed it to the King.*

*Meres spoke as the King placed the ring upon her finger.*

*"This ring symbolizes the circle of love that will last forever."* The King smiled at Esther.

Meres reached for the solid diamond tiara and handed it to the King. *"You may crown your Queen."* Esther lowered her head slightly and the King gently placed the tiara upon her head.

*"You may now seal this marriage with a kiss,"* stated Meres.

The King and Queen touched lips briefly and turned to face the crowd. All clapped and cheered. The King and Queen walked down the aisle. The two servants immediately grabbed her train as she began to walk toward the crowd. When they reached the front steps of the wedding hall, Haman had two beautiful black stallions draped with velvet and gold trim around the horses. They were attached to a chariot that had wheels studded with gold.

The body of the chariot was richly embroidered with royal symbols and pastel colors. An elaborate parasol that shaded the carriage was ready for their ride through town. When the King and Queen reached the chariot, the servants removed the bridal train off the wedding gown. The King aided Esther into the carriage, and then he climbed in and sat closely to her. Haman led the procession through the Town Square.

The wedding guest went to the ballroom where the feast was being held. The procession started, Mordecai stood among the crowd and hoped to catch a glimpse of Esther or that she might see him.

The King and Queen smiled and waved to all the people of the town. Esther tried to find her uncle, but as she rode through the streets filled with faces and waving arms, it was difficult to see him. They rode through the cheering crowd for a few minutes before returning to the palace ballroom for the feast. When the King and Queen entered the ballroom, the guests cheered and applauded again.

*"Thank you, thank you, all my honored guests. Please, eat and drink all you desire,"* insisted the King.

*The King and Queen made their way to the head table. "Esther would you like a goblet of wine or something to eat?" asked the King politely.*

*"A goblet of cool water and some fresh fruit would be delightful, my King."*

*"Servant!" cried the King. "A goblet of cool water and some fresh fruit for my wife."*

*"At once, your Majesty." The servant left quickly.*

*"My Queen, I see some fellow countrymen I haven't seen in quite some time. I'm going to speak with them for a few moments. I will be right back."*

*"Yes, of course. Take your time my husband."*

*The King kissed Esther's hand and went to speak to some of his fellow Kings and Noblemen. While he held conversations with different Kings and Noblemen of his provinces, minutes passed. The King glanced around the ballroom full of colorful crowns and beautiful gowns for his friend, Mordecai. With all that he had done for the King, surely time spent for his wedding would not have been too much for Mordecai to consider. The King continued to look around the crowd, he saw Haman. The King gradually moved through the crowd smiling and nodding to fellow noblemen until he reached Haman. His back was to the King. The King tapped Haman on the shoulder. "Haman," said the King.*

*Haman turned with a goblet of wine in one hand, a turkey leg in the other and a mouth full of food. "Did you send an invitation to Mordecai? I do not see him here. I would have imagined he would have come."*

*Haman completely caught by surprise, almost choked on the food he was eating. He immediately took a sip of wine to wash down the clogged food in his throat. His heart began to beat faster as he regained his breathing.*

*"Ahhhh, my King, Mordecai said he couldn't make it. He had a prior engagement." Haman was still trying to swallow his food.*

*"Prior engagement?" asked the King, in disbelief, "What could be more important than your King's wedding?"*

*"He didn't say your Majesty," said Haman, regaining his composure.*

*"Ohhhh, my goodness!" explained the King, "I know, I bet I know why he didn't come."*

*"Why is that, Sire?"*

*"Mordecai has a daughter. He probably didn't come because I didn't invite her too. I should have invited them both. That's just the kind of man he is, family first. Well, thanks Haman. I must make my way back to my new bride now." The King started to walk away, but he turned to speak to Haman again. "Oh, by the way Haman, excellent job on security." The King left Haman and started to make his way through the crowd.*

*Haman wiped the sweat balls from his forehead that had formed while he was talking to the King. However, Haman saw how easy it was to deceive the King.*

*Soon the King reached the head table.*

*"I apologize Esther, for being gone longer than I had planned. I just started talking about battles and wars and time went by."*

*"It's ok, I've been speaking with some of the wives and I find we have a lot of things in common."*

*"Yes, you are all married to Kings," he laughed. Esther smiled.*

*The hours passed quickly, guests began to leave. The King and Queen bid every guest farewell as they left the ballroom. The sun had begun to shine brightly for the next morning when the last guest walked out of the ballroom door. "My King. The hours have been long. I am very, very tired. May we retire for this morning?"*

*"Yes, my Queen. Let's get some rest and start a new day as King and Queen of Shushan." They left the ballroom exhausted. They slept for the rest of the day.*

# Chapter 5

## *Esther as Queen*

*As the day grew late, they both had rested. They went to the dining room where they waited to be served dinner at the six o'clock hour. The King and Queen enjoyed a lovely dinner alone that evening and many mornings and evenings to come. However, after months of learning the King's mannerisms and observing the staff, one day Esther decided to make a special request of the King as they sat at the breakfast table.*

*"My King, I would like to go among the town's people to let them meet their Queen and let them speak with me if they like. Does this meet with your approval?"*

*"But they saw you on our wedding day," said the King.*

*"I know, Sire. But they did not speak to me."*

*"If you wish, my wife. But take Haman or have Haman send some guards with you. But, I don't really see what purpose this would serve, Esther. It has been written in the decree that you would be my Queen and now that we are married, it's a fact. The people will obey you whether they like it or not," stated the King firmly.*

*"My King, you cannot know what the people are thinking if we do not speak with them," explained Esther softly.*

*"I am King, Esther. What does it matter what they think? They do as I say, as do you," the King stated with authority.*

*"Yes, my husband, I mean no disrespect to you. I wish only that the people may see and know of their new Queen. I promise my King, I will do nothing to bring you dishonor or disrespect to the King's throne. Also my King, may I take food to give to the people?"*

*"What food? Where do you intend to get the food from Esther?"*

*"From the palace storage room, my King."*

"*This is absurd. Just what do you hope to gain by giving food to the peasants?*" asked the King, uncertain of Esther's motive.

"*I wish to gain nothing, my Lord. Only to let the people know that we are a caring King and Queen.*"

"*We are royalty, Esther. You don't need to be in the village with peasants.*"

"*These peasants are you Kingdom, your Majesty. Let's show them we care for them,*" Esther said softly.

"*Very well, Esther. Go! But do not let me hear of dishonorable acts by you.*"

"*You have my word, my Lord and I thank you.*" Esther bowed to the King. She left the room.

The King called to Esther to remind her again.

"*Take Haman and some guards with you to walk among the people.*"

Esther turned and bowed again.

"*Yes, my King.*"

Esther walked from the King's sight.

"*Obtisse!*" cried Esther, as she walked down the corridor.

Obtisse hastened her footsteps to meet the Queen.

"*Yes, my Queen, you summoned me?*"

"*Go to the kitchen and gather some food. We are going to ride through the town. I want to let the people know that their King and Queen care for them.*"

"*My Queen, have you permission from the King to take the palace food?*" said Obtisse, surprised at the request.

"*Yes and we have plenty. It will never be missed. Go now and gather as much as you can. I must find Haman and have him escort me through town.*"

"*Yes, my Queen.*" Obtisse scurried away.

Esther saw Haman looking over the palace balcony.

"*Haman!*" called Esther.

"*Yes, my Queen,*" said Haman. He turned around to greet her. He bowed.

"*I am going to ride among the people today. The King insisted that I take you with me for security.*"

"*My Queen, before you make such ventures, you must give me time to prepare for your safety. I do not think this is a wise idea right now. The people may not receive you with a warm welcome, even though you are Queen. Can you postpone this activity until I can pick some of my best guards to handle this situation?*"

"*No, Haman, I cannot. I have the King's permission to ride into town and either you take me or I will find someone who knows how to follow orders. As for the people receiving me with a warm welcome, that is what I intend to find out,*" *Esther spoke softly.*

*Haman fought to conceal his anger with no facial expression.*

"*Very well, my Lady,*" *he responded,* "*I will take you and I will pull three of my best guards away from their duties to assist me.*"

"*Thank you Haman, you are kind indeed,*" *Esther smiled.*

"*Do you want a carriage or a horse prepared for your ride through town?*" *asked Haman.*

"*A horse. It will be easier for me to meet the people face to face by climbing off a horse than climbing out of a carriage.*"

"*As you wish, my Lady.*"

*Haman turned from Esther and motioned to a guard to come forth that was posted in the corridor.*

"*Guard!*" *yelled Haman.*

*The guard immediately responded to Haman's call and stood at attention in front of him.* "*Yes, Chief Haman,*" *said the guard.*

"*Have Adak send me three well trained guards, four horses and the Queen's royal horse. Have the horses posted in front of the palace in ten minutes.*"

"*At once,*" *stated the guard. He dashed off to relay the order to Adak.*

"*Who is Adak?*" *asked Esther.*

*"Adak is my second in charge, my Queen."*

*"Why have I not met him yet?"*

*"You will today, I keep him very busy my Queen,"* stated Haman.

At that moment, Obtisse walked up accompanied by two cooks carrying two huge baskets.

*"My Goodness! My Lady and just what do you intend to do with all that food?"* asked Haman.

*"I intend to distribute it to some of the people in town."*

*"I know the King did not approve of this! Feeding the hungry with the King's flour and grain from the kitchen...that's absurd,"* cried Haman.

*"Nonsense,"* replied Esther, *"We have plenty. I know I can't feed the entire town with just two baskets of food, but it's a start. Now, have your guards to carry the baskets and we shall go."*

*"I will not!"* Haman firmly insisted, *"My men's hands must be free to protect your..."* Haman realized he was speaking to the Queen and immediately lowered his voice, *"To protect you, my Queen. You must bring a servant along to carry these baskets."*

*"Very well. Obtisse find some other servants to carry the baskets."* Just then, three armored guards with swords reported to Haman. Haman raised his right hand, a motion for the guards to stop. The guards paused behind Haman and awaited further instructions.

*"I will do better than that, my Queen. Have the guards bring the baskets to the rear of the kitchen,"* instructed Obtisse.

*"You heard her Haman. Have the guards bring the baskets to the kitchen,"* ordered the Queen.

Haman angrily mumbled a few words trying not to be heard by the Queen.

*"Guards take these baskets to the rear door of the kitchen,"* commanded Haman.

Everyone went to the kitchen. Obtisse was already at the rear door.

"*A donkey?*" *cried Haman, "Where did we have such a creature?*"

"*Never mind, Haman,*" *said the Queen, "We must be on our way. Have the guards place the baskets on the donkey.*"

"*You heard the Queen men, place the baskets on the donkey.*"

*The donkey had a basket carrier on his back. The guards secured the baskets on the donkey. One basket on each side.*

*Just then one of the guards spoke to Haman.*

"*Chief Haman.*"

"*Yes.*"

"*Adak wanted me to inform you that the horses were prepared for travel in the front of the palace.*"

"*Very well. Bring the donkey to the front of the palace soldier.*" *The guard nodded in recognition of Haman's command.*

"*Let's go my Queen,*" *said Haman, "The horses are ready. If you will follow me.*"

*They all headed toward the front of the palace, even Obtisse. Once they opened the front door, Adak bowed. He was holding the Queen's horses in position for travel.*

"*Your horse, my Lady,*" *said Adak.*

*Esther saw Adak for the first time. He looked as muscular and tall as Haman did. Esther noticed her horse had a saddle so well polished and decorated with royal ornaments that it glimmered in the sunlight and could be seen from yards away. A delightful difference from riding bare back with her Uncle Mordecai.*

*The other guards took their positions, two guards in the rear, the Queen and Obtisse in the middle, Haman and one guard in front. One of the guards in the rear pulled the donkey along.*

*The procession began a slow trot through town, the people cheered that were mingling about the town square. When suddenly, in a short distance, Esther saw an old woman that she knew from her trips to the well.*

"Haman stop," called the Queen. Haman stopped and turned around on his horse to see what the Queen wanted.

"I want to get off my horse and speak to that old woman sitting by that building." Esther pointed. Haman looked in that direction.

"Very well, my Lady." Haman dismounted his horse and assisted Esther off hers. "There you are my Queen."

Esther walked toward the old woman. She sat next to an old adobe building. Haman followed the Queen. The old woman appeared to be tired about the face. Her hair was totally gray and uncombed. Her skin had lots of wrinkles that depicted her many years of age. The clothes she wore looked like rags that hung off her skinny body. "My lady how are you these days?" asked Esther.

"I'm trying to make it, my child. But each day seems to be a little longer than the next," mumbled the old woman with no teeth.

"I understand."

"I know you understand, Queen Esther, you've walked these paths before. But do not forget where you came from," muttered the old woman.

"I have not my lady, for I have brought food for as many as I can feed."

"Bless you my child, as you have always had a good heart. You would speak to me and bring me water from the well when others would look the other way."

Haman grew weary of this little reunion. He was repelled by the sight of the old woman.

"Once the King finds out about you talking to peasants, he will be very displeased," said Haman. Esther ignored him.

"Well, today my lady, you can have some bread and some water from the well." Esther turned from the old woman to speak to Haman.

"Haman, tell Obtisse to bring me a loaf of bread." Esther turned back to the old woman. "Pass me your pouch and I will *fill it."* The old woman passed Esther her water pouch that she kept by her side.

*"Obtisse! Bring a loaf of bread for the old woman,"* shouted Haman.

*Obtisse was assisted by a guard off her horse, she then pulled a loaf of bread from one basket and hurried to hand it to the Queen. "Here my Queen." Obtisse handed Esther the loaf of bread.*

*"Take this pouch Obtisse and fill it at the well for me."* Obtisse took the pouch and walked to the well. It was only a few feet away. One of the guards walked with her.

*Esther reached to hand the old woman the loaf of bread. The old woman grabbed Esther's hand. Haman quickly raised his arm to slap the old woman with his hand across her face. The old woman saw Haman's action and immediately released Esther's hand. She dropped the loaf of bread to the ground, closed her eyes and shielded her face with her hands, expecting to receive a harsh blow from Haman. Esther saw the old woman react. Esther turned and noticed Haman with an arm raised.*

*"Stop! What are you doing!" yelled Esther at Haman. Haman stared at the old woman and lowered his hand from Esther's command.*

*"Peasants are not allowed to touch royalty," explained Haman.*

*"She is a person, not a peasant and she has my permission to touch me!"*

*Haman restrained his anger and turned his back to the old woman.*

*Esther reached down to pick up the bread the old woman had dropped. She gently pulled the old woman's hands down from her face and placed the loaf of bread in her hand. The old woman opened her eyes to find a smile on Esther's face. She smiled too. The old woman again reached for Esther's hand to lay a kiss upon it. Esther leaned down to kiss the old woman on the cheek and she placed a soft hand on the side of her face. The old woman smiled again. By this time Obtisse had returned from the well with the pouch of water.*

*"Here you are, my Lady," Obtisse handed Esther the pouch. Esther turned and handed the pouch to the old woman.*

*"Bless you, my child," mumbled the old woman.*

*"Take care my lady and bless you." Esther turned from the old woman to go back to her horse. Haman followed.*

*"My Queen I must insist that we refrain from any further charities and return to the palace," protested Haman.*

*"Haman you have your orders from the King. You may go back if you wish, but I'm going on!" replied Esther, tired of his negative attitude.*

*Haman appeared stressed. His face turned flush and veins appeared on his forehead. However, he controlled his anger.*

*"Your safety is my job. I will follow you, my Queen," Haman quietly replied. At that moment, Esther turned from Haman only to see the girls she had met so often at the well.*

*"Bow down to your Queen!" Haman shouted to the girls.*

*The girls kneeled before Esther. "Rise," said Esther to the four girls. As each girl stood, especially, Porthea, Esther reached for her and firmly embraced her. "All is forgiven." Esther smiled at the girls, and then she continued her ride through town. The girls bowed and watched her ride away.*

*Esther continued to give all the food she had brought with her away to as many people as she could. Hours later, the procession finally returned to the palace.*

*"Those people are peasants my Queen and you should not be among them. It would not do you well to partake upon this adventure again. Only for your safety my Queen, do I say this," said Haman.*

*"I will take it under advisement," said Esther, "I have no further need of you Haman. You are excused."*

*Haman bowed and left the room to find the King. Esther remained in the kitchen for a few moments. Haman entered the throne room. "My King!" called Haman.*

"What is it? Is Esther all right?" the King asked, concerned that something may have happened to Esther.

"Yes, my King, the Queen is fine. But she did an unusual thing today, which had me confused."

"And what was that, Haman?"

"She gave flour, grain, and bread to the peasants of the town," explained Haman.

"Was that to gain favor with the people?" asked the King.

"No my King, the people already liked her and she knew some of them."

"Haman, whatever the Queen orders you to do, you will do. Understood?" the King spoke firmly.

"Yes, my Lord."

At that moment, Esther walked into the throne room. She bowed to the King.

"You may go now Haman," ordered the King.

Haman left the room. Esther and the King watched him leave.

"Esther, why didn't you tell Haman I gave you permission to take the food to the peasants?"

"I didn't think it necessary, my King. I apologize."

"Only because he is security, my darling and I want you safe at all times."

"Yes, my King."

"Esther, Haman does have a point. We cannot go through the town giving our food away to the peasants. It's just not safe."

"My King, if this displeases you, I will discontinue taking food into town. But, my husband, the people were so grateful. You should have seen the smiles on their faces. It brought joy to my heart."

"This made you happy, Esther, feeding peasants? Diamonds, rubies and gold I can understand making you happy, but feeding peasants?"

"Yes, my King, very happy. I felt like I was doing something to help the people."

"*Esther, feeding peasants is not the Queen's position. However,*" the King said softly, "*If this makes you happy, keep the feedings to a minimum and let's not go into town. Please.*"

"*Yes, my Lord. I will not go into town to feed peasants. I'm tired. I think I will retire for the evening, if the King permits.*"

"*Yes you may, and I shall retire with you, Esther.*" They both left the throne room together. He held out his arm and Esther placed her hand upon his.

The remaining daylight faded into dusk and Esther had a restless night. She was up long before the King. She went into the kitchen. The servants were preparing a King's breakfast.

"*My Queen,*" said Harbonah, "*How may we serve you this morning for breakfast?*"

"*The King does not like for me to go into town among the people sharing the palace food. He is very concerned for my safety. Therefore, I want you to go and gather some of the children from the town and bring them here so they might be fed, Harbonah.*"

"*Fed! Fed from the King's kitchen! Forgive me my Lady,*" cried Harbonah, head cook. "*Your intentions are honorable, but the King will be angry.*"

"*The King is a kind and understanding King. You know, Harbonah, I couldn't sleep last night. As I rode through parts of town that I had never seen before, I saw children with their mothers starving and begging for food. How can I just ignore that when I am in a position to help them? Our kitchen is bursting with food. Now go, please and bring some children for morning breakfast.*"

"*As you wish, my wonderful Queen,*" said Harbonah. He exited the kitchen door.

A long time passed. Harbonah honored the Queen's request and gathered children from town to eat breakfast at the palace.

"*Here you are, your Highness,*" announced Harbonah. He pointed to the children. Esther gazed into the slightly dirty faces of the little children as they clanged tightly to their mother's dress.

71

*"Fifteen children are all you could find?" asked the Queen. Harbonah looked shocked, eyebrows raised and mouth open. He said not a word.*

*"Never mind," said the Queen, "Set the table and feed the children and their mothers." The other cooks had breakfast prepared.*

*"Please sit down and eat." Esther smiled politely at the children. The women gingerly set their children around the huge oblong table. The servants set plates of food before them.*

*"Thank you, Queen Esther, you are too kind," said one mother, while she spooned eggs slowly into her child's mouth.*

*"What if the King finds out, my Lady?" asked another child's mother.*

*"Then he finds out. What everyone doesn't seem to understand is that our King has a kind and loving heart. He loves his people," smiled Esther.*

*"But not in his kitchen," muttered Harbonah underneath his breath. Not to be heard by the Queen.*

*"Harbonah, make sure they get enough to eat, I will be right back."*

*Esther left the kitchen through one entrance and the King, followed by Haman entered through another.*

*"Well, I'll be boiled in oil!" exclaimed Haman in disgust, "How did all these peasants get into the kitchen without my guards stopping them?"*

*"What is the meaning of this, Harbonah?" demanded the King.*

*Esther heard the angry voices of Haman and the King. She immediately raced back to the kitchen.*

*"Haman get these peasants out of my kitchen, now!" the King demanded. He pointed angrily at the mothers and their children.*

*"I'm just as astonished as you are, my King. But I promise you; I will get to the bottom of this."*

*Esther dashed into the kitchen through the entrance from whence she had left only moments ago.*

"I beg of you my King, let the children and their mothers at least finish their breakfast and I promise they will leave. I will see to it," begged Esther.

The King looked at the saddened eyes of the mothers and their children, he turned to Esther.

"Esther, you had these peasants brought to our kitchen?" asked the King softly.

"Yes, my King, I did," Esther spoke softly with a bowed head.

"Very well, Esther, they may finish their breakfast. But, how did you get them pass the guards?" asked the King.

Haman listened closely.

"One of the servants knew some of the guards on watch and they let them in because I asked." Esther glared into the King's eyes with the innocence of a small child.

"Very well, come and see me at the throne room after you finish here, please, Esther," said the King with a mellow voice. Esther bowed to the King. He immediately turned to Haman. "Haman come with me," said the King.

"Yes, my Lord," said Haman. The King and Haman departed the room.

"I am so sorry, all of you, for the inconvenience I have caused. Please, finish your meal and do not rush. I will explain what I did to the King."

"Yes, my Lady," said Harbonah, "I will see to everything here."

"Harbonah, it seems to be a problem for me to go into town or to have the poor families come to the palace. I feel that the King doesn't mind giving the poor people food when I suggest it. It's just that he doesn't want me, personally to do it. So, the only other solution I can think of, is to have you go out on occasion and deliver the food with the King's signed permission. What do you think?" asked Esther.

"My Queen you are too kind. But, if it is your desire and with the King's permission, I would be honored to deliver food to *the poor." All the mothers smiled. "Thank you Harbonah. Now I must go and see the King."*

*Esther left for the throne room. Moments later, she stood before the King.*

*"Esther," said the King softly. She bowed when she entered the room. "Why did you not tell me you were going to invite peasants to our kitchen?"*

*"Feeding peasants is not a Queen's job," added Haman. The King and Queen both looked at Haman with anger in their eyes. "You may leave us, Haman!" shouted the King. Haman bowed to the King and Queen and exited the room.*

*"I did not think you would care, my King. I did not go among the people as you stated. I thought you were only concerned with my safety among the people. So I thought if I brought them here, my safety would not be an issue."*

*"You know, Esther, you brought the people here, without consulting Haman for security reasons or me. He is Chief of Security. Your safety and mine is his concern. He must be made aware of who comes and goes in this palace. I know your heart is in the right place, Esther. But we still need to let our servants do their jobs," firmly spoken by the King.*

*"Are you angry, my King?" Esther spoke with a mellow voice and almost tearful.*

*"I was, at first, Esther. But I can see now that you just have a soft heart. A heart that I am learning to love more and more each day. Since you've been here, you have only concerned yourself with others. The beauty of your heart is unmatched by any women I have ever known. I do love you, Esther." The King's tone of voice rose slightly, "But we must refrain from bringing people in the palace unannounced to me, or Haman, right?"*

*"Yes, my Lord and I am sorry. That will not happen again."*

*"Come and wrap your arms around me, I want a big hug," said the King lovingly. They hugged each other tightly and exited the throne room.*

## Chapter 6

### The Decree

*Haman, feeling rejected by the King and Queen was on his way home when he saw Mordecai outside the palace gates. He stared at the palace walls on occasion hoping to get a chance to see Esther, just to see if she was doing alright.*

"What are you doing here Mordecai? The palace is off limits to you. Unless you care to kneel at my feet."

*Mordecai turned away from the palace walls and stared into Haman's eyes.*

"Are you not a man like I am a man? Is the blood red that runs through our veins? Do we not eat, drink and walk alike? You are no better a man than I, Haman, and I kneel down before no man," *softly spoken by Mordecai.*

"I am the King's second in command and nothing goes in or out of the palace without my approval. That makes me better than you!"

"Believe what you will Haman. God judges both of us whether you believe in Him or not. I kneel only before God. I will not kneel before any man. Now please, don't ask me again, Haman," *stated Mordecai mildly.*

"Or what Mordecai? What will you do?" *shouted Haman. Mordecai looked away from Haman and back at the palace walls.* "Just as I thought, nothing. Be gone from here Mordecai! The King will see you no more and I will just as soon see you dead! Go home, you good for nothing Jew. This is the last time we will speak in this manner." *Mordecai mounted his horse and rode home. Haman watched Mordecai leave with fury in his eyes and hatred in his heart. Haman had enough of Mordecai's disobedience. Now was the time to reveal his plan. Haman quickly returned to the palace in search of the King.*

"My King! My King!" *Haman shouted,* "There is a group of people that are traitors to the King."

The King had left Esther in bed from her tiring day. Haman met the King in the corridor.

"What do you mean, Haman?" whispered the King, "Lower your voice. The Queen is resting. Let us go to the throne room and discuss this further." They walked toward the throne room, Haman continued with his news.

"I have gotten word from sources that are my eyes and ears among the people, that the Jews do not consider you as their King, but some King they call Jehovah," said Haman.

"Jehovah? Who is this King called Jehovah?"

"The Jews believe he is a powerful King, much greater than you."

"Greater than me? That's treason!" shouted the King.

"His army is mightier than yours and they worship him, not you. We must eliminate the Jews before they poison the minds of all your people."

"Eliminate?" restated the King. "That's so final. We are talking about thousands of people."

"Yes, my King. We must destroy them! Squash them! Kill them! Until no more of them exist to spread any more traitorous words about you." The King thought about what Haman had spoken. He paced the floor for a few moments.

"Yes, you are right Haman. If what you say is true, it must be stopped now! Upon sunrise tomorrow, come back and have my scribes write a decree sending the Jews into exile for blasphemy."

"Exile?" said Haman curiously. "Did you hear what I just said, Sire? The Jews are talking treason."

"Yes! Haman, exile! Do you have a problem following my orders?" the King stated angrily.

"We kill traitors, your Highness!" Haman said aggressively.

"Haman, these people may not believe in me, so let them go without food or water to be with their so-called, Jehovah. He will take care of them. When they are starving and thirsty, they will know who their true King is and they will come crawling back to me for forgiveness."

"But, Sire, if we kill them, you don't have to worry about them crawling back to you."

"Enough talk! I have given you an order. Exile them! Or you will find yourself a guard instead of second in command. Now go!"

"Yes, your Majesty." Haman smiled and bowed to the King. He left the throne room angry.

Haman felt the King was weak. He was too weak to be King. He was going to fix the decree to suit his desires. He had deceived the King once before, one more time will not make a difference. However, he did not want to tell his wife that he had fallen short of getting rid of Mordecai. Haman mounted his horse. He galloped on rocky roads and cut through tall trees to reach home quickly and alert his wife of the wonderful news. Darkness fell upon his arrival at the front door.

"Zeresh I have done it!" He shouted excitedly, "Tomorrow the King will sign a decree to eliminate Mordecai."

"How wonderful, my dear! Then have the master builders build a gallows so high that all the Jews may watch what happens to a disobeying Jew," said Zeresh.

"I will instruct the master builders to do so. However, it's not just for Mordecai. It's for all Jews. I can't wait my darling wife. Soon Mordecai will stand up to me no more."

"Instead he will die before you, my husband and all the other Jews as well," smiled Zeresh.

"Yes. Him and thousands of other Jews," Haman added.

"Let us retire wife, I have a big day tomorrow," smiled Haman.

The hours passed slowly and before the morning light, Haman couldn't sleep. He rode back to the palace before sunrise. Haman met with the scribes and the master builders. The scribes wrote the decree and the builders would start immediately on the gallows.

Haman couldn't wait to give the decree to the King. He waited in the King's study for hours. Later, that morning the King entered his study room.

*"Haman, what are you doing here so early?" asked the King.*

*"I have received the decree from the scribes, it is ready for your signature, Sire."*

*The King sat down to his desk, Haman placed the decree before the King. He fought to conceal his nervous, for he had changed the content of the King's decree. He was talking fast to distract the King.*

*The King glanced at the decree when Haman laid it before him.*

*"This decree will stop anyone else from thinking that they can be traitorous to the King," said Haman, " I have read it three times myself. I assure you everything is in order."*

*"Very well, Haman." The King trusted Haman to have followed his proclamation to the letter.*

*The King reached for his quill, dabbed it in a small ink jar and signed the decree without reading it.*

*"Very good, your Majesty," smiled Haman.*

*"Here Haman, the decree is signed. Place my seal upon the decree with the ring that I have given you and send it throughout all provinces. Traitors will not be tolerated in my Kingdom."*

*"I shall see that this decree is passed throughout all the provinces. Every valley and household shall hear of it. We will leave no stone unturned, my King." Haman bowed to the King with the decree in his hand and immediately exited the room. Hours later, the decree was posted on buildings throughout Shushan. A day later the decree was throughout all 127 provinces.*

*On this particular day, Mordecai was brushing his horse, tending the sheep and cleaning house. He was sweeping the dust out of the kitchen into the front yard, when two neighbors approached.*

*"Mordecai!" cried Tabor and Esam. They raced to his front door. "Mordecai!" They cried again.*

*"What is it? What's wrong?" Mordecai was startled by the cry of his name.*

"*A great mourning and wailing has gone out throughout the town among all the Jews,*" *shouted Tabor.*

"*Why?*" *Mordecai asked, shocked at the news.*

"*You haven't seen the decree that is posted throughout the town?*" *asked Esam.*

"*No. I have been working at home all day. Decree? What decree are you talking about?*" *Tabor handed Mordecai the decree they had taken off a building in town. Mordecai read silently.*

"*How could the Queen, your so-called daughter let this happen?*" *Esam asked, angrily.*

"*Only two people can issue a decree in this kingdom and that's the King and Haman with the King's permission,*" *said Mordecai.*

"*That's right Mordecai. This decree, signed by the King, plans to eliminate all Jews in one week. What do you say about that, Mordecai? How could Esther let this happen?*" *asked Esam.*

"*Do not fear my brothers. This is not the work of the King. This is the work of a man filled with hatred and anger, Haman. I am sure my darling Esther knows not of this decree or she would have questioned the King. I will have a word with her.*"

"*How? You said yourself, Haman will not let you near the palace gates,*" *asked Tabor.*

"*Have faith my friends, God is with us always. If you do nothing more, pray for our safety. I will ride to the palace at once to try and speak with Esther.*"

*Without hesitation Mordecai dropped his broom and climbed on his horse. Mordecai rode to the palace immediately and waited for dusk to fall. He waited in front of palace gates behind some shrubbery, until finally Mordecai spotted a servant leaving from the palace.*

"*Servant,*" *Mordecai whispered.*

*The servant tried to stare through the darkness, but saw no one. "Where are you?" asked the servant. He looked around in every direction.*

"*Shhhhhh...*" *whispered Mordecai. "Here behind these bushes." The servant walked closer to the bushes, tentatively and fearfully, not knowing what to expect from someone that needed to hide.*

"*Who's there?" the servant asked, softly.*

"*Come behind the bushes, quickly before someone sees you.*"

*The servant glanced around to see if anyone was alerted to his actions. Cautiously he crept toward the beckoning voice.*

"*I know you," whispered the servant, surprised to see whom it was. "You are Mordecai, friend of the King. I remember you when you came to visit Hazor. The King said you saved his life. I overhear these things going about my duties in the palace. Why are you hiding? I'm sure if the King knew you were here, he would be glad to see you.*"

"*Servant, listen, and listen carefully. You must get this message I have written to Queen Esther immediately. Time is of grave importance. Please, let no one else look at this but the Queen. Please," said Mordecai, anxiously.*

"*As you wish, I will take it to her now," said the servant.*

"*Thank you, thank you so very much," said Mordecai, "I will be right here until she gives me a reply.*"

"*Very well," said the servant.*

*Mordecai peered from behind the bushes, looking toward the palace walls. Then he turned to the servant. "The way is clear, go, now." The servant quickly left from behind the bushes. Modestly, he walked toward the palace.*

"*Open the gates!" shouted the servant to the guards. He approached the palace walls. The guards on the wall knew the servant.*

"*Hatach you just left, why are you back so soon? Did you forget something?" asked the guard.*

"*Yes, I did, Pular, could you be the good friend that you are and open the gates for me, please?" stated Hatach. He held the message behind his back.*

"Open the gates!" shouted Pular. "Don't make this a habit." Pular smiled, "I have better things to do than open and close gates for you." Hatach smiled, walked through gates and waved. He returned quickly to the palace. He found Queen Esther in the living room. Hatach held the message along with a copy of the decree in his hand.

"My lady," cried Hatach, "I have a message for you from a man named Mordecai. He is hiding behind some shrubbery in front of the palace. He asked me to give you this." Hatach handed Esther the message and the decree. "He seemed most disturbed."

"Disturbed? Hatach?" Esther took the message and the decree.

"He said it was imperative that you get this message right away."

"Thank you," said Esther. She began to read. Hatach and Obtisse watched her expression with deep concern. Tears began to form in her eyes and run down her cheeks. She began to read aloud the last few sentences of the message.

"How could the King sign such a violent action as to annihilate an entire race of people, that has done him no wrong? This has got to be the work of Haman, my darling Esther. Haman has promised to pay a King's treasure to all that would help destroy the Jews. Somehow you must right this wrong. You are a Jew too, my dear. If the King truly feels this way, it would only be a matter of time before you would die as well. You must go to the King and reveal to him your heritage."

Esther glanced up from the letter. Her eyes were red from fallen tears. She looked at the decree, one sentence Mordecai had underlined and she read.

"All Jews, women, children, babies and males must be killed for traitorous acts against the King." Esther saw the King's signature and the seal in total disbelief.

"How horrible, my Queen," frowned Obtisse. "How could the King sign such a decree?"

*Danielle James*

"I must go to the King and tell him the truth. That I am Jewish too." Esther's lips and voice quivered.

"No, my Lady, the decree is for the death of all Jews. The King will surely end your life as well," warned Obtisse.

"I cannot stand by and do nothing." Esther went to her desk, reached for a quill, ink and paper. "Obtisse, you and Hatach see that this message gets to Mordecai. She wrote... Dear Uncle, I will go to the King and tell him the truth. But, I need you to do one thing for me. Tell the people to fast and pray for three days, for on the third day I will go to see the King and tell him I am Jewish. I love you, may God be with us. Esther."

"Are you sure my Queen that you want to do this? If you go to the King on your own and he did not call for you, it would mean your life. In order for your life to be spared, the King must hold out the golden scepter for you to approach him. That is the only way," cried Obtisse.

"If I do nothing, it could mean my life anyway if this decree is carried out." Esther handed the message to them, "Go quickly, Obtisse and Hatach to deliver this message to my uncle. I shall prepare myself for the King." Obtisse and Hatach bowed to the Queen and exited the room immediately.

Esther went to her bedroom alone. Thoughts raced through her mind. Did the King knowingly sign the decree? If so, why? How could she convince the King to rescind the order? But more importantly, how could she stop the executions in time? Still in tears, she kneeled by her bed with both hands together. She began to pray.

"Lord, my life is devoted to You and only You. I have tried to do what is right for others and not just for myself. I am asking You now Lord to give me the wisdom and the courage to take this challenge and meet it head on. My life is in Your hands, may Your will be done. Thank You, Lord. Amen."

Esther rose from her knees and lay across her bed to rest. Esther rested peacefully. Hours later, she heard a knock at her door.

82

"Come in," said Esther softly. Obtisse gently pushed the door open and bowed to Esther.

"Your command has been honored Queen Esther and your uncle's reply was, the fast by the people shall be done."

"Thank you Obtisse."

"What are we to do now? Your life would be in danger if you went to see the King on your own accord?"

"I know. I have been in prayer and for hours I have been in thought of ways to handle our situation. I have a plan. I believe it will work and I'll need your help."

"Yes! my Queen, anything."

"Here is what I want you to do? Prepare three beautiful dresses for me to wear over the next three days. But, I will wear the most beautiful of them all on the third day."

"What do you have in mind my Queen?" asked Obtisse, inquisitive of her plan.

"You will see, Obtisse. First take this decree my Uncle Mordecai gave me and hide it in the kitchen where you can find it. Alert the cooks not to touch it if they see you."

"Why?" Obtisse asked, with a puzzled look on her face.

"Please, no questions now, we must act quickly. It will all make sense later. Now do as I ask and come back here after you have finished."

Obtisse took the decree and hurried to the kitchen. As she entered, Harbonah was preparing the week's dinner menu.

"Harbonah, I must hide this decree for the Queen. Where is a safe place?"

"Here, Obtisse, give it to me." Harbonah took the decree.

"Look, Obtisse, I'm placing the decree in this large sack of flour and I am marking the sack with an "X". I will alert the other cooks not to touch this particular sack. It will be safe. As Chief Cook, I will see to that."

"Thank you, Harbonah."

"If I can be of any more assistance, please ask. I'll do anything to help my gracious Queen."

83

*"Ok, my friend, if we need anything we will ask. Thank you, again."*

*Obtisse left the kitchen and returned to Esther's bedroom.*

*"It is done, my Queen."*

*"Good. Next, have Ababa to come and fix my hair in a different style everyday for the next three days, starting tomorrow. Now, go and prepare."*

*"Yes, your Highness." Obtisse bowed and left the room.*

*The hours passed and the evening grew late, Esther could not sleep. Esther continued to pray.*

*"My Lord, this is a terrible decree that has fallen upon my people. If a life must be shed, then let it only be mine. Thousand need not die for one man's hatred of another. Please, God, give me the words, the wisdom, and the courage to stand and fight this battle. Amen."*

*Suddenly, a peaceful calm fell over her. She rested well after her prayer. She knew the Lord was with her. As the sun glared through the palace balcony, Esther awoke from her sleep ready for the difficult task ahead. Suddenly, she heard a knock at the door.*

*"Come in."*

*Obtisse entered first, with a dress draped over her arm.*

*"How beautiful!" cried Esther, admiring the gown.*

*Ababa entered with a tray loaded with perfumes, make-up and hair ornaments.*

*"Excellent!" smiled Esther, "Now, ladies, it's time to go to work."*

*That day, Esther placed on one of her best dresses and wore the finest of perfumes with her hair beautifully styled.*

*"You look like a Queen," joked Obtisse.*

*"I just hope the King will think so too. If you will excuse me, I must let the King see me." Esther walked toward the throne room where she knew he would be at this hour of the day. Esther walked down the corridor and elegantly paced in front of the throne room where the King could see her from a distance. Esther did this throughout the day.*

*The King noticed her, but she was too far away for him to get her attention. Esther went back to her bedroom where Obtisse and Ababa waited to hear what had taken place.*

*"Did you see the King?" asked Ababa.*

*"No," said Esther.*

*"Why not, my Queen?" asked Obtisse, baffled as to what Esther actually did.*

*"I don't want to speak to the King today, not just yet."*

*"My Lady, why don't you tell the King at dinner time or bedtime what Haman has done?" asked Obtisse, "You know during the day he is very busy with other Kings and Princes or his staff."*

*"Obtisse I want to catch Haman off guard. If I alert the King to what Haman has done, the King would confront Haman, alone."*

*"But that's what you want, isn't it?" said Obtisse.*

*"Yes it is. But it might give Haman an opportunity to lie his way out of the situation. Blame it on someone else. I don't want that. I want him to be totally surprised. So shocked, that he doesn't have time to think of a lie. So his only alternative would be to tell the truth in front of the King."*

*"Yes my Queen, but why wait three days?"*

*"Timing is everything, Obtisse. Today I aroused the King's curiosity. Tomorrow when he sees me he will be curious and concerned. But, I don't want him to know just yet what is wrong. By the third day, he will be so anxious to know what I want, that I will have his complete and undivided attention. His desire to know, will supercede any meetings or prior engagements. His full attention will be focused on the situation that I present to him."*

*"I understand, my Queen," said Obtisse, "It sounds as if you thought this all out very carefully."*

*"I have. Obtisse, thousands of thousands of lives are at risk, especially little children. They will die and for what? One mans prejudice of another. No! Obtisse, that is why I cannot make a*

*mistake or lives will be lost. I must be careful on how I approach the King."*

*"You're right, my Lady. But you said yourself, the King is a kind and understanding King."*

*"Yes Obtisse, he is. But if I approach him the wrong way, I can run the risk of making him angry. And I don't want the King to think that I am attacking a member of his staff for no reason."*

*"Ok my Queen, I'm ready. Let's go ahead," said Obtisse. Ababa just stood there and listened. She knew the Queen was right. "I'm ready too my Lady," said Ababa firmly. The second day arrived. Obtisse brought another beautiful dress and Ababa was ready to perform her duties with the make-up and perfume. Hours later, Esther was dressed.*

*"Obtisse where is the King? Is he in the throne room as usual? Do you know?"*

*"Yes, my Lady, the King is in the throne room and Haman is with him."*

*"Great! I'm glad Haman is there too," stated Esther.*

*"You look nervous my Lady. I beg you not to do this," Obtisse stated, concerned for Esther's life.*

*"I am fine. I'm not nervous, just anxious," Esther stated with confidence. She held her head high and looked toward the heavens. "Be with me, Lord."*

*At that moment, Esther lowered her head and a sudden calm came over her. Her face was without expression. She began to walk down the corridor, this time, much, much closer to the throne room.*

*Esther heard two men talking from afar. "Haman, I noticed gallows being built in a distance. Why is that?" asked the King, moving about the throne room. He looked from the ledge of the palace window.*

*"Ahhhhhh, Sire, ahhhhh, the gallows are for cutthroats and thieves. This will perhaps make them think twice before committing a crime."*

*"Good!" stated the King. When he turned from the window, the King saw Esther again in the corridor.*

*Haman smiled boldly. He had deceived the King once more.*

*"You know, your Highness, this decree you have signed will remove all doubt in the kingdom as to whom the people will bow to. These Jews have no respect for authority."*

*"Yes, yes, Haman," said the King, bored with the conversation. His eyes were still focused on Esther in the corridor.*

*"My King, perhaps we should move the date up to exile the Jews."*

*The King was curious to why Esther was in the corridor a second day.*

*"No Haman, let things stand as they are."*

*The King maintained his focus on Esther. She continued to pace the corridor. The King's curiosity was intensified. He reached for his golden scepter that lay on a small table beside his chair.*

*"Excuse me, Haman. Esther!" called the King, "Come here!"*

*Esther gracefully walked into the throne room. The King held out the golden scepter for Esther to touch. She touched the scepter and kneeled before the King.*

*"Rise. How beautiful you look, my darling. Doesn't she look beautiful, Haman?"*

*"Yes, my King." Haman bowed when she entered the room. The King held out his hand to Esther. She took his hand. He led her toward the throne. The King sat beside her. "You are dressed beautifully, my wife. I noticed you yesterday in the corridor. I would have called you, but, I was meeting with King Rafda on important business. I meant to ask you last night what was bothering you, but my thoughts were elsewhere. You have been pacing the corridor for a couple of days, now. Something troubles you Esther. Tell me what is it so that I may help solve the problem."*

*Esther glared at Haman, then looked back at the King. "Tell me what troubles you Esther. That I may take care of it for you," said the King, concerned. Haman stood a short distance from them.*

*"Yes, my Queen, if there is something or someone that is troubling you, let me know and it will be disposed of immediately. Your wish is my desire," said Haman.*

*Esther stared at Haman with no expression on her face. She then looked back at the King.*

*"My King, my husband, if I might have dinner prepared tomorrow evening for you and Haman. I shall reveal my thoughts then, that you both may help."*

*"Why tomorrow? Tell us now and it shall be dealt with now! My love," insisted the King.*

*"Tomorrow, my husband and I trust you will make it back tomorrow Haman?" asked Esther coyly, as she stood from her chair.*

*"Promptly, my Queen." Haman bowed.*

*"Good, we will see you at six Haman," said Esther, " If you will excuse me, my King." She bowed to the King and exited the room as gracefully as she entered.*

*"I am deeply confused, Haman. What is on her mind?" asked the King.*

*"It is perhaps nothing my King. You know how some women are, they may need more gowns or perfumes. Do not worry my King."*

*"Haman you are probably right. You are excused for this day. I will see you at dinner tomorrow."*

*"I will go home and give the news to my wife. I am more than honored to be your dinner guest tomorrow, my King."*

*Haman bowed and left the throne room.*

## Chapter 7

## *The Fall of Haman*

*Haman rode his horse with the speed of the wind to reach his home. He finally felt confident that he was getting the reward he desired. Hours later, he entered his house. His wife greeted him at the door. "Zeresh! I am an honored guest of the King and Queen. They invited me and only me to dine with them tomorrow at six."*

*"This is surely a promotion my husband. I will tell our ten children their father is standing on top of the world and we have every reason to be proud of him."*

*"Everything is going my way, my darling. In less than one week the Jews will be no more and no more Mordecai. I tried to get the King to push the date up, but he wouldn't hear of it."*

*"Why?" Zeresh asked, curiously.*

*"He seemed bored with the conversation about the Jews. He was more occupied with watching Queen Esther pace up and down the corridor. I'm not sure he heard a word I said, after he saw her."*

*"Do you think the King really wants to do this? Kill the Jews I mean?" asked Zeresh.*

*"It doesn't matter my darling, I'm doing it."*

*"What do you mean?" asked Zeresh.*

*"I had the scribes to write the date and words I wanted on the decree. The King wanted two weeks, I said seven days and the other alteration was to kill the Jews instead of exile them. I did it without the King's knowledge."*

*"What! How did you manage that?" Zeresh asked, curiously surprised.*

*"Well, I just told the scribes that this is what the King wanted, seven days. Since I said to place the word traitor in the decree, the scribes knew that traitors are killed. So they did not question what I told them to write. They just worded everything*

Danielle James

to read well. They had no reason to doubt me. I'm second in command. I hold the ring with the King's seal. I'm the man in charge of everything!" Haman smiled.

"Are you out of your mind? Are you crazy!" Zeresh stated, angrily.

"What do you mean? I thought this is what you wanted," Haman stated, confused at the tone of her voice.

"It is, but with the King's permission! What you have done is altered a decree signed by the King. That's treason! You may have brought the gallows down on yourself, rather than Mordecai."

"Do not worry yourself, woman. I know what I am doing."

"It would have been easy just to get rid of Mordecai. You could have had him to mysteriously disappear. The King would have never noticed one man gone. But, no, not you. Chief of Confidence! You have got to kill thousands of Jews. Without the King's permission! The gallows are almost finished. I have seen them. Just what do you propose to tell the King when he asks you, why are you hanging people everyday?" Zeresh sarcastically stated.

"Don't give me this honesty look. You want me to be in power as much as I do. What I have done, I have done for our family. Look at our home. It's beautiful, but we can have so much more. Don't fall apart on me now, wife. I need you in my corner."

"But, how could you change the decree? What were you thinking, Haman?"

"Well, I ran into Mordecai on my way home and he still refused to kneel before me. I was furious. I'd had enough. I immediately went back to the palace to find the King. My initial intent was to just get rid of Mordecai, but when I started thinking to myself, it progressed into killing all the Jews. The more I thought, the more it sounded like a great idea."

"Now you are going to kill an entire race of people because of one man?" said Zeresh.

*"The King wouldn't do it when I asked him to. He's weak. He didn't have the heart to kill them, so I had to. And besides, why are you so negative? What do you care about the Jews? I thought you would be pleased at my efforts?"*

*"Only if your efforts didn't place a noose around your neck."*

*"Zeresh, King Ahasuerus is so in love with the Queen, he can't think straight. He let's her get away with anything. The other day she took palace food to the peasants. Another day she brought the peasants to eat in the palace kitchen and what does he say? "That's all right, darling. That's fine." And what does he tell me? "Do whatever she says."*

Haman paced the floor as he explained. *"She's more concerned about doing for others than she is for the King. That's it!"* Haman had a thought. *"That's got to be it. She's inviting me to dinner so she can tell me something nice she's doing for me."*

*"It's got to be that promotion, right?" asked Zeresh.*

*"That's right, wife. So I need you on my side. Don't abandon me now. Not in my moment of triumph."*

*"I'm not sweetheart. I just hope you haven't gone too far with the authority you have been given," Zeresh said softly.*

*"You said it yourself. I'm resourceful. I have the King in the palm of my hand. He trusts me without question. Killing the Jews won't be a problem. I'm so smart, that after the Jews are out of the way, our weak King will be next," stated Haman with confidence.*

*"Just be prepared, Haman. I say again, what do you intend to tell the King when he sees those gallows going up?" asked Zeresh.*

*"The King believes in me and trusts me with his life. I told him the gallows were for cutthroats and thieves. He believed it. Whatever I tell him, he will not question. I have deceived him several times before, but this time will be our victory."*

*"I just hope you know what you are doing," Zeresh spoke, tenderly.*

*"Just trust me my darling wife. Once the Jews are killed, the King will be next on my list and we will be sitting on the throne, Queen Zeresh," Haman stated with a smile.*

*"If what you have done, husband, comes to pass, I will love you always," admired Zeresh.*

*"Let's drink a glass of fine wine to celebrate this great occasion," boosted Haman.*

*"I just happen to have some on the table in the kitchen."*

*They went into the kitchen. Haman took the top off the wine bottle while Zeresh got the glasses.*

*Haman poured the wine in both glasses. "A toast," said Haman cheerfully, "Death to the Jews." They both took a sip of wine.*

*"A toast, to your promotion my darling and more power and money to our family," said Zeresh.*

*They both took another sip.*

*"I'm too excited to eat, I'm just going to call it a day and get some rest," said Haman. As the night fell, they finished their wine and Haman and Zeresh retired for the evening.*

*That same evening, the stars glowed in the darkness of the sky. Esther gazed upon them from her balcony bedroom. The King walked up behind Esther. He placed both hands upon her soft slender shoulders.*

*"Esther, it hurts me to know that something is troubling you." Esther turned around to address the King.*

*"I will let you know tomorrow, my love," said Esther, "Let's get some rest, it's been a long day."*

*They laid down to rest, the minutes and hours passed. And again, the bright sun lit the sky for a new day.*

*Haman arrived early at the palace. He spoke to one of the guards. "I must ensure that all goes well this day" instructed Haman, "Make sure no one comes to see the King unless I know who it is first."*

*The guard nodded his head in recognition of Haman's command.*

Meanwhile, Mordecai was still lurking on his knees behind the bushes, awaiting any word from Esther as the third day had arrived. Suddenly, someone crept up behind Mordecai.

"Mordecai," said Tabor. Mordecai turned to see Tabor standing behind him.

"Shhhhh, not so loud," Mordecai whispered. He rose from his knees.

"Mordecai, the word has been spread and the people have done as you asked them to do. They have fasted and prayed for the past two days and even now as we speak," whispered Tabor. Mordecai grabbed Tabor's arms with both hands and smiled.

"That's wonderful my friend. Now we are all in God's hands," said Mordecai, "We will know by tomorrow whether the decree will be enforced or rescinded." Mordecai lowered his hands. "Go now my friend and don't worry, I will bring word once I know what has happened."

"Yes, Mordecai, we will await your word. May God be with you and the Queen," said Tabor.

Tabor departed quietly. Mordecai knelt back down in the bushes and waited for time to pass.

The evening drew near. The six o'clock dinner hour finally arrived.

"Haman," cried the King. He spotted him coming down the corridor. "You are right on time. Come into the dining room. The Queen will be in shortly. Please sit. Servant!" A servant entered the room quickly from the kitchen. He bowed. "Bring two goblets of wine." The servant bowed without a word and went swiftly from the King's command.

"Is this some kind of surprise celebration or a promotion for me, my King?" asked Haman, "I am honored to be in the presence of my King and Queen, but the anticipation has left me with a sleepless night."

"We will soon find out what the desires of the Queen's heart is for you Haman. Be patient. I am sure she appreciates all that you have done to keep her safe from harm and this may be her way of rewarding you."

*The servant brought the two goblets of wine. He placed the goblets before them.*

*"Will that be all, your Majesty?" asked the servant.*

*"Yes, you are excused," said the King. The servant exited the room.*

*"Drink some wine Haman and enjoy the evening," said the King.*

*The King peeked impatiently down the corridor.*

*"Ahhhhh, here she comes now."*

*Haman rose from his seat and placed his goblet of wine on the table.*

*Esther entered the room in the most beautiful dress she had ever worn and Obtisse trailed her. Haman bowed.*

*"My Queen," said the King, "We are about to partake in a goblet of wine. Would you care for some?"*

*"No thank you, my King," said Esther.*

*"My Queen you look lovely this evening," adored Haman.*

*"Yes darling, you do look astoundingly beautiful this evening," added the King.*

*"Haman and I were just speaking of why you invited just him to dinner. Would you please tell him, so that he might drink and eat without worry."*

*Esther smiled at the King. "Yes my King and Haman, let us go to the dinner table and be served."*

*"After you my Queen," said the Haman. He motioned with his arm to the dining room table. Haman picked up his wine goblet. He motioned for the King to follow. But the King aloud Haman to go first. So he followed the Queen. The King followed after Haman.*

*"Obtisse, is the table prepared?" asked Esther.*

*"Yes, the cooks are ready to serve, my Queen," said Obtisse.*

*Soon they reached the dining room table.*

*"Haman," instructed Esther, "You will sit here on the right side of the King and I will sit at the other end of the table."*

*The King took his place at the head of the table.*

*"Obtisse, have the servants bring the food," said Esther.*

*Obtisse bowed and went into the kitchen.*

*"Esther won't you please tell us what this is all about?" impatiently, asked the King.*

*"My husband, the cooks have prepared pheasant, fresh fruit, potatoes, corn, turkey and much, much more for our dinner. Let's eat first, please."*

*The King sighed and so did Haman.*

*Moments later, the servants brought the food and set it before them.*

*"Hmmm, how wonderful this food looks. It is truly a feast set for a King," admired Haman. He glanced at the King and Queen with a smile.*

*"Tell the servants what you want to eat Haman," said King Ahasuerus. Haman looked at the food.*

*"Very well, give me a little bit of this and a little bit of that. Well, I'll take some of everything."*

*"And for you, my King," said Esther.*

*"I'll have some turkey, potatoes, and fruit," said the King to the servants. The servants set the plates of food before them.*

*"My darling," the King asked concerned, "Aren't you eating?"*

*Esther glanced at Haman. Haman was looking at his plate of food.*

*"Haman," said the Queen.*

*Haman raised his head from his plate.*

*"Yes my Queen," replied Haman. He looked at the Queen curiously.*

*"You are the King's right hand man. Are you not?" asked Esther.*

*"Yes my lady. I would lay down my life for you and the King," replied Haman with a slight note of nervousness in his voice.*

*The King was puzzled also. "My wife," asked the King, "Are you questioning Haman's loyalty to us?"*

*Haman took a couple of sips of wine. His heart began to beat a little faster than normal.*

"Yes, my King," Esther said firmly. Haman rose sharply from the table and looked at the King, then back at Esther.

"My Queen, what have I done to offend you? I would lay down my life a thousand times to protect yours or the King's," explained Haman, his tone bordering desperation.

The King rose briskly and looked at Esther. She was still seated at the table. "What is going on Esther? Tell me now! What has Haman done to warrant this questioning?" asked King Ahasuerus in an aggressive tone of voice.

"You, my King, have signed a decree to kill all Jews in the Kingdom," said Esther, calmly.

"What?" said the King angrily, "What are you talking about, Esther? Yes, I signed a decree to exile the Jews and that was because Haman said they were traitors of the Kingdom. But what does that have to do with you my darling?" asked the King.

Haman stared at Esther.

Esther glared at Haman. She rose from the table.

"You see Haman, I am a Jew." Haman was startled. "I am the niece of Mordecai. The man you hate so much. He raised me from six months old. My uncle taught me that life is precious. It should be savored, not destroyed."

Haman backed away from the table. His eyes widened, jaws dropped and his hands trembled. He dropped his wine goblet to the floor and he fell to his knees. Sentences became difficult to say. "My Queen I, I, I, did not know." He looked at Esther, then turned to face the King, "My King I did not know. Please don't, don't kill me. I am sorry. I apologize. I, I, I, didn't know! Please forgive me," Haman's pleading face turned from the King to the Queen.

"Silence! Haman," said the King. He turned to Esther, "Esther the decree I signed was to exile, not kill the Jews. Where are you getting this information from?"

"Obtisse!" called Esther.

"Yes, Queen Esther."

"Bring the decree."

*Haman appeared extremely nervous. Obtisse returned to the kitchen to retrieve the decree from where Harbonah had hidden it. When she noticed, Harbonah was standing in the middle of the kitchen floor with the decree in his hand. He had been listening to the entire conversation.*

*"Obtisse I have prepared the decree for the King's review. I would be honored if I may walk with you back into the dinning room. I would like to see justice done." He handed Obtisse the decree.*

*Tension mounted in the dinning room, Obtisse and Harbonah returned quickly with the decree. Obtisse handed Queen Esther the decree.*

*"Here, my Lady." Esther took the decree and walked toward the King.*

*"Here my King, here is the decree that has been posted throughout all the provinces."*

*The King took the decree from her and read it silently to himself. While he read, Esther explained the circumstances.*

*"My King, if this decree is carried out, that all Jews must be destroyed, then I must take my place with my people and my life must end too," said Esther, solemnly.*

*"My signature! My seal!" The King looked at Haman with fire in his eyes. He took his wine goblet from the table and smashed it to the floor with one hand and crumbled the decree with his fist in the other.*

*"My King!" cried Esther, "If blood must be shed, then let it be mine and mine alone." The King's eyes were focused on Haman.*

*"Haman! You altered my words and sealed the decree with my ring. I trusted you. How could you betray me? You are the traitor! Not the Jews!"*

*Esther walked closer to the King and laid her hands upon his shoulder, a sense of calm began to return to the King as her touch soothed his angry temper. The King turned to Esther and a smile appeared. He reached for her, he held out his arms and*

*Danielle James*

*Esther gazed into his eyes. She embraced him. The King looked into Esther's eyes.*

*"You are the love of my life and I have known only happiness since you have been my wife. Your kindness and joy has brought peace and harmony into the palace. No harm shall ever come to you as long as I am King."*

*The King released Esther and turned toward Haman. "As for you Haman!"*

*Haman still on his knees, spoke before the King said another word.*

*"My, my, my King, have mercy upon my soul. I, I, I meant the Queen no harm. I didn't know! I would gladly give my, my, my life for hers, my King. I, I didn't know!"*

*"Silence! Haman. Give your life, will you? Then that you shall."*

*"My King," cried Harbonah, "Look at a distance through the window. The gallows that are built are for the Jews to be hanged. And thirty pieces of gold to all that assists in eliminating the Jews. This is the word on the streets of Shushan, your Majesty."*

*"What? Another lie!" shouted the King, "You told me...never mind." The King lowered his voice. "You built those gallows for the Jews and promised thirty pieces of gold to all that would help you in killing the Jews?"*

*Haman nodded, still on his knees. He lowered his head close to the floor.*

*"Haman you have mounted a threat of death against my wife, you have lied to me about the Jews, and you have dishonored me by changing my decree without my consent. What is the penalty for what you have done?" Haman raised his head from the floor.*

*"I would send me into exile, your Majesty."*

*"I'm sure you would from where you are kneeling right now. Look through the window, Haman, the gallows you built for the Jews shall be used for you and your wife. Guards!" shouted the King.*

"*Noooo! my King! Not my wife,*" screamed Haman, pleading on his knees.

"*You should have thought of that while you were plotting to kill my wife.*"

"*I didn't know she was a Jew.*"

"*If you had not tried to deceive me by altering my orders, your neck would not be in a noose. Guards!*" explained the King. The guards came quickly into the room.

"*Take Haman to the dungeon, where he will remain until his day of reckoning!*"

"*At once, your Highness,*" said one of the guards.

"*Stand and walk out like a man,*" said the King to Haman. Haman reluctantly stood. The guards gripped Haman by the arms.

"*Hold out his right hand,*" said the King to one of the guards.

"*I'll take that ring, Haman,*" said the King, "*Where you are going you won't be needing it.*" The guards escorted Haman to the dungeon.

The King turned to Esther with a smile. He reached again for her and they embraced. "*I am sorry Esther. I would have never signed such a violent act. But, I promise you this, no one shall ever come this close to hurting you again. I shall pass another decree tomorrow revoking the elimination of the Jews. As for Mordecai, your uncle, you say? I will appoint him as the King's Advisor to my Army as well as Chief of the Guards. Does this please you, my wife?*" asked the King.

Esther gazed lovingly into his eyes.

"*My Lord, this pleases me,*" Esther smiled.

"*Let's retire my darling wife, you have had an exhausting day.*"

They walked to the bedroom, the King held Esther around her waist and her head rested upon his arm.

The hours passed by and the night fell, the dawn of a new morning glimmered through the balcony of the palace. Esther awoke, only to find the King was not at her bedside. She placed her robe on only to find the King had been up for hours in the throne room.

"Esther as you slept, I had my scribes prepare a new decree to be spread throughout the land, sparing the lives of all the Jews." At that moment, a knock came at the door, Mordecai entered the throne room. Esther's eyes glowed with happiness. She smiled at the King lovingly. "I also had Mordecai brought to the palace to take his place as Chief of the Guards and the King's Advisor." Esther raced toward Mordecai and embraced him.

"You see Esther, your prayers and actions did not go unnoticed by God," stated Mordecai.

Mordecai and Esther walked over to the King. Esther kissed the King on the cheek. Mordecai shook the King's hand and as he did so, the King placed the ring in his hand that Haman had held for so long.

Esther looked at the King and tears came into her eyes. "Thank you, my King. You have filled my heart with joy, as you promised," said Esther.

All three walked toward the balcony to look out over the Kingdom. Esther lagged behind her two favorite men.

King Ahasuerus and Mordecai stood on the balcony. "Why didn't you come to your own niece's wedding? I sent you an invitation. I thought you didn't come because of your daughter, not knowing Esther was whom you were speaking of."

"Invitation?" asked Mordecai, "I never received an invitation. If I had, I assure you I would have been there."

"But, Haman told me...never mind." The King remembered whom he was speaking of.

"You raised her well, Mordecai, Chief Advisor. I want you to know I love her very much. She is a beautiful lady inside as well as out."

"I love her too, my King," added Mordecai. Esther glanced at the King and Mordecai standing on the balcony, she looked to the heavens.

"Thank you, God!" smiled Esther.

# *Chapter 8*

## *The Plot*

*Esther walked up to join her two favorite men. They gazed over the balcony at their Kingdom. When Esther approached the King, he reached for her hand and gently pulled her toward him.*

*"My darling Esther, you shall have the house of Haman and all therein," said the King.*

*"Thank you, my King. If I may, I would like to give the house to my uncle.*

*"It's yours to do with as you desire."*

*Esther turned to Mordecai. "Uncle you may have the House of Haman for your own domain."*

*"Thank you my Queen," Mordecai bowed.*

*Esther smiled. It felt strange to have her uncle bowing to her in her honor. She reached for Mordecai and gave him a gentle hug. She then turned to the King and kissed him on the cheek.*

*"My King, I feel great today! I'm going to the kitchen and have Harbonah prepare a King's breakfast," said Esther with a smile.*

*"Very well, Esther." Esther bowed and left the room. The King turned to Mordecai.*

*"Mordecai, I have a few things to discuss with you."*

*"Yes, my King."*

*"Mordecai, today I want you to bring Zeresh, Haman's wife, to the dungeon to join her husband in his fate today and remove their ten sons from their home."*

*"I didn't realize Haman had ten sons to follow him. I can't take his house. Where will the boys go, Sire?" asked Mordecai, concerned.*

*"I don't know and it's not a concern of mine where they go. If you don't take the house, I will sell it. But they will leave that house. Explain to them what their father has done to bring this*

*tragedy upon their family. You should take several armed guards with you, as I am sure they will not go without a fight."*

*"Yes, your Highness."*

*"Also Mordecai, I had the scribes to write another decree to change what Haman had done. They should have finished it by now. Will you take a look at it and see if it's to your desire? If not, feel free to change or write what you deem appropriate to get the message across to the people that the Jews are not to be harmed. Then you may seal the decree with the King's ring. I trust you, Mordecai."*

*"Thank you, your Majesty. I will take care of it." Mordecai bowed and started to leave the room.*

*"Oh! Mordecai," the King called, "It must be done today. In two days the executions are to take place."*

*Mordecai turned to face the King. "It will be done at once, Sire." Mordecai left the throne room.*

*The King placed his arms behind his back, hand in hand, walked over to the window and gazed at the morning sunrise as it settled upon his Kingdom. At that same moment, several miles away, Zeresh awoke from her sleep to find herself alone. Haman was not lying beside her. She immediately put her robe on and frantically searched the house to find him. Finally, minutes later, she stood in the middle of the living room trembling with fear and anxiety.*

*"AAAAAAAAAAAA, Noooooooooo, AAAAAAAAA!" she screamed to the top of her lungs."*

*Her sons, startled from their sleep, raced from their upstairs bedrooms. They dashed down the stairs to the living room, wrapping their robe belts tightly around their waists. Once they reached the living room floor, their mother was waving her arms hysterically in the air, jumping and screaming around the floor. The oldest son, Dalphon, a dark curly haired young man, with broad shoulders, reached her first.*

*"What's wrong, mother?" asked Dalphon, excitedly. He tried to grip her with his strong masculine hands.*

*Zeresh resisted. She continued to scream and holler standing in the middle of the floor. By this time all the sons had reached her. Three of them grabbed her about the shoulders to aid Dalphon in holding her still. Dalphon shook her to stop the screaming.*

*"Mother! What is it?" asked Dalphon, curious to the reason for her emotional outburst, "What is it?"*

*She gazed into her son's dark brown eyes. He held her tightly about the shoulders. She looked at him with a blank expression upon her face and suddenly tears formed in her eyes.*

*Again, Dalphon asked pleasantly, "What is it, mother? Please tell me," he pleaded, setting her gently on the couch. He sat beside her holding her hands. The other nine brothers gathered around.*

*"I fear the worse for your father, Dalphon. Your father went to the palace last night for supper at the Queen's request and he has, not returned." Zeresh stared straight ahead, with no expression.*

*"Ohhh, mother, is that all?" casually said Arisai, her second oldest son, with light brown hair and a slender build. "Father just probably got a little drunk and decided to sleep in the guard's quarters before coming home."*

*Zeresh's blank stare was broken by the words of disbelief that something had happened to their father. Tears stopped flowing. She sniffled. Dalphon handed her a white cloth from his robe pocket.*

*"You don't understand my children," she explained. She dried her cheeks. She sniffled, "Remember I told you your father was about to be Chief of the King's Army, plus Chief of the Guards, more money was going to be coming into the house and he had found a way to eliminate the Jews and everything was just great?" she excitedly stated. Zeresh looked around into the concerned faces of all her sons.*

*"Yes, mother," said Parmashta, her third oldest son, with black hair and long sideburns. He stood tall with a huge masculine chest and muscular arms.*

103

*Danielle James*

*"Well, your father did some things he shouldn't have done,"
Zeresh regained her composure.*

*"Like what, mother?" asked Parmashta, his dark brown
eyes locked intensely upon his mother.*

*"Your father altered the King's decree from exiling the Jews
to killing them."*

*"You mean the King didn't want to kill the Jews?" asked
Aspatha, her seventh son, with dark brown hair and a medium
build.*

*"That's right, my son," said Zeresh.*

*"That's treason!" shouted Arisai.   At that moment, there
came a knock at the door.  Adalia, the youngest son, medium
height, with long dark black hair brushed slickly behind his ears,
raced toward the door.*

*"It's Adak and the King's guards!" shouted Adalia.*

*Zeresh and Dalphon rose from the couch.   The guards
entered the house.  They were fully armed with swords and body
armor.   They wore helmets of steel and held shields in their
hands.  They appeared ready for battle.  Adak, the leader of the
soldiers, stared at Adalia when he walked into the house.*

*"Why are you looking at me so hard?" asked Adalia.*

*"How did you get that scar on your chin?  That wasn't there
the last time I saw you," said Adak.*

*Before Adalia could reply.*

*"How dare you enter our house at this hour of the
morning!" shouted Dalphon.*

*"Dalphon.  Not so bluntly.  Adak is our friend," said Zeresh
pleasantly, "Why have you come Adak?"*

*"Zeresh," Adak began calmly.  He removed his helmet and
placed it underneath his arm, "I do not come as a friend this
time.  I am the bearer of bad news."  Zeresh clinched Dalphon's
arm with both hands.*

*"And what news is that Adak?" asked Zeresh, fearing the
worse.*

104

"*We have orders from the new Chief of the Guards and by the King's command that we escort you to meet your fate with Haman.*"

"*New Chief of the Guards!*" *shouted the sons in unison.*

*Zeresh tighten her grip on Dalphon's arm.* "*Meet my fate, is that a polite way of saying...*" *Adak interrupted calmly.*

"*Yes, Zeresh you are to be put to death with your husband.*"

"*Noooo!*" *her sons shouted.*

*Zeresh fainted. She fell limp in Dalphon's arms. He laid her on the couch. All the sons were shaking their heads and uttering the word no. They gathered about their mother to revive her. Dalphon walked closer to Adak.*

"*Can we speak for a moment Adak?*" *The two walked away from the guards and the other brothers. Dalphon conversed alone with Adak.*

"*Adak, you have known my father and mother for years. You have shared our food right here in this house. You are father's best friend and right hand man. How can you come in his house and take his wife, my mother, to be executed? You know her like a sister. Do you know what you are doing?*" *asked Dalphon, frustrated.*

"*Dalphon, I'm just following orders. Not only are your parents to be executed, but you and your brothers are to leave this house immediately. You have until tomorrow to get out.*"

"*What! Why is this happening?*" *asked Dalphon.*

"*According to Mordecai, the new Chief of the Guards...,*" *said Adak.*

"*Mordecai!*" *screamed Dalphon, interrupting Adak. He remembered his father saying the name before.* "*The Jew that disrespected father.*"

"*Yes, Mordecai. Your father deceived the King by altering a decree that was sent out to kill the Jews. Well, the Queen is a Jew and Mordecai's niece.*"

"*My goodness, Adak! I'm sure father had no idea the Queen was Jewish.*" *Dalphon paused and paced the floor.* "*Let me think.*"

*Danielle James*

Adak, the guards, and Dalphon's brothers watched him nervously pace the floor. The brothers wondered what they were talking about as they still tried to revive their mother by patting her cheeks and hands. Minutes passed.

"Adak, what would it take for you to look the other way and let my mother and us leave Persia. I promise, you will never hear from us again."

"Nothing young man. If I let you leave, I'd better be right behind you. I have a wife and a family to think of. The King would have my head. No Dalphon, we must take your mother and you and your brothers must leave this house by tomorrow."

"You won't help me?" asked Dalphon, he felt rejected.

"Not this time. It's my life if I help you." Adak moved back from Dalphon. "Guards!"

"Nooooo!" shouted Dalphon, he clinched his fist and swung violently at Adak. Adak dodged the swing and pushed Dalphon to the floor. Two guards raced to hold Dalphon down. The other brothers started to react to the action that was taking place between Adak and their brother. Several guards jumped in between the brothers, showing shields and swords to impede their progress to reach Dalphon.

"I'm sorry, Dalphon. Guards hold him to the floor." Adak turned to the other guards. "Hold the other brothers back and take her!" Adak motioned to three other guards to carry Zeresh to the horse that awaited her outside. Adak looked at Dalphon. The guards held him with his arms behind his back. The other guards started to carry their mother outside. She was still unconscious. Her sons screamed and shouted while struggling to break free of the guards, but with no success.

"Stop, Adak!" screamed Dalphon. "My mother didn't have a part of this. Why?"

"King's orders!" shouted Adak.

"Don't take my mother!" shouted Adalia with anger in his eyes.

"Don't take our mother!" the other sons screamed repeatedly, with the sound of fury. The guards ignored all the screams and shouts of unpleasant words and carried out their orders.

"Once you have secured her for travel, take her to the palace. The rest of us will stay here and ensure they don't follow," stated Adak to his guards. The guards took Zeresh and quickly exited the house.

"Adak, how could you?" asked Dalphon. He struggled to break free from the guards, to no avail. The other brothers, extremely angry, watched the guards remove their mother from the couch. They fought the guards with greater intensity for their freedom to save their mother, but there were just too many guards holding them back. Adak waited a long time before he freed the young men from the barricade of guards that held them captive.

Adak drew his sword from his sheath and pointed it at Dalphon. "Release them!" He shouted to his guards.

"This is not the end! Adak," Dalphon shouted, rising to his feet.

"Dalphon you know what must be done. Do it! Or we will be back to do it for you!" stated Adak firmly. Adak and the rest of the guards, with swords drawn, backed their way out of the house. As soon as they heard the rumbling of horse hooves, in a distance, the brothers ran out of the house. All the brothers stood on the front grounds, they stared at the dust that flew behind Adak and the guards.

"Quick! Let's get our horses and weapons and ride after them. Four of you go to the stables and get the horses. The rest of you, let's get the weapons from the house. We won't take this insult smiling. Let's move!" demanded Dalphon.

Dalphon and his brothers went back into the house to retrieve their swords, while the other brothers went to the stables. On their way back outside to pass out the weapons.

"The horses are gone!" shouted Adalia, the first one to reach the stables, "Not one horse is in the stables."

"They released the horses," stated Parmashta to Dalphon solemnly.

"This means war upon the royal palace." Dalphon spoke aloud, "Gather around brothers." All the brothers gathered around and waited until the rest of the brothers made their way back from the stables. Soon all the brothers stood before Dalphon.

"Take your swords, my brothers," said Dalphon to the other four that had just come from the stables. The brothers took their swords and sheath and affixed them to their waist.

"What did Adak mean by what he said? "You know what you must do." What did he mean by that Dalphon?" asked Arisai.

All the brothers looked to Dalphon for the answer. Dalphon stared with fire in his eyes down the trail that the soldiers had taken their mother.

"What Adak meant was, we have to leave this house by tomorrow or they will be back to help us move out," said Dalphon.

"What!" shouted the brothers in unison. The loud explosion of disbelief in his brother's voices broke the trance Dalphon had upon the trail that appeared long and distant. He gazed into the eyes of his brothers.

"This house isn't our home anymore?" asked Aspatha.

"That right, it's now the property of the palace," said Dalphon.

"What are we going to do?" asked Arisai.

"We are going to avenge our parent's deaths. This should have never happened. Our father wouldn't have wanted their lives to go uncontested. We will all vow to our last breath to kill Mordecai and the Queen for the executions of our parents. Do you all promise that you will give your life to avenge their deaths? I do!" shouted Dalphon.

Dalphon stared at each brother. They all responded in agreement, except Aspatha.

"Before we go seeking revenge on Mordecai and the Queen, do you want to tell us what just happened here? I think the rest of us need to know why soldiers abducted our mother from her home, our father is being hanged and we are being tossed out of our home," asked Aspatha. *"Could you enlighten us, please?"* The rest of the brothers turned to Dalphon again. *"You heard mother say that father altered the King's decree to kill the Jews instead of sending them into exile, as the King ordered."*

*"Right. Why did father alter the decree?"* asked Aspatha.

*"Well, father didn't know the Queen was Jewish when he did it,"* said Dalphon.

*"The Queen is Jewish?"* asked Parmashta.

*"That's right. She is Mordecai's niece. Mordecai is the Jew father hated for disrespecting him, by not kneeling before him. Father altered the decree to strike back at Mordecai,"* said Dalphon.

*"The Chief of the Guards is the uncle of the Queen?"* asked Aspatha.

*"Ohhhhh, my goodness!"* said Arisai. *"The Queen's a Jew, Mordecai's a Jew, and who knows, the King could be Jewish too, for all we know."* All the brothers were stunned.

*"Now do you agree to avenge your parents death, Aspatha?"* asked Dalphon, *"We need to round up the horses and move out."*

*"Wait, hold on,"* cried Aspatha. *"Father was wrong in altering the King's order. Has anyone thought about that? We don't need to get back at royalty. What father did was wrong."*

*"Just a minute, little brother. You're one of the youngest of us all, what do you know about what father did and didn't do?"* asked Dalphon.

*"I know what father did was wrong. I also know that this is not the first time that father has deceived, lied, cheated, or stepped on others for his own personal gain,"* said Aspatha.

*"What are you saying? You know of something else?"* said Arisai.

*"Yes."*

*"Well, enlighten us little brother,"* spoke Dalphon.

*"It was late one night, a couple of years ago, before father became Chief of Security at the palace. I came down stairs late one night to go out front for some fresh air, I couldn't sleep. A*

*light was burning in father's study room. I went to see who was up besides me. As I approached the door, I heard two voices. One was father's voice and the other was of a man I had never heard before. I didn't want father to know I was there. So I didn't make my presence known. I listened for awhile to hear what they were saying."*

*"So what did they say?" asked Arisai.*

*"Apparently, father wanted the job of Chief of Security very badly," said Aspatha.*

*"Why do you say that?" asked Dalphon.*

*"Father and Adak were the two most qualified soldiers to get the job of Chief of Security if something should happen to Hazor. Father wanted to be the only one qualified for the position. What the two of them were discussing was how to discredit Adak to seem less capable of following orders in front of the King and Hazor. By discrediting Adak, father would be a better choice for the job."*

*"What!" shouted the other brothers in amazement.*

*"Alright!" shouted Dalphon, "So you knew father wasn't the most honest man around. That's still no reason to kill him or mother."*

*"Forgive me big brother, but father, of all people knew what the laws were. He knew to change the decree, an order of the King's, without the King's permission was treason. You break the law, you pay the penalty," said Aspatha. All the brothers grew angry with Aspatha for what he said.*

*"Whose side are you on?" asked Arisai.*

*"How about the right side?" said Aspatha.*

*"You mean we should let our mother and father hang without revenge on those who caused their deaths," said Dalphon.*

*"My brother, did you hear what I said? Father caused their deaths. Father lied and cheated his way to the top. And knowing father, the King might have been next on his list of people to get rid of."*

"Well, I didn't hear you crying, father we shouldn't live in this big beautiful house, or father we shouldn't have all these nice clothes and things, or father we should give all the food we have to the poor. You didn't care how father got the money or whom he stabbed in the back to get it. You overheard that conversation and you said nothing. Not even to father," said Parmashta.

"I admit, I'm guilty too. I saw it happening and let it take place," said Aspatha.

"So stop trying to be the righteous one. We are going to take over royalty and win. I will not let my father and mother die for a bunch of Jews or Jew lovers!" said Arisai.

"Don't you understand? Killing the Jews isn't going to bring mother and father back to us. Let's just pick up the pieces and try to get our own lives in order," said Aspatha. Dalphon visibly angered by the words his little brother had spoken, struck Aspatha across the cheek with his fist. So forceful was the blow, it knocked him to the ground.

"Little brother, I don't want to hear another word from you. Either you are with the rest of us or you are on your own. Which will it be?" demanded Dalphon, while he stared at his brother on the ground.

Hostility mounted, with all the brothers in agreement with Dalphon, while Aspatha lay face down on the ground.

"Let us know now! Are you with us or not!" shouted Arisai. Aspatha spit dirt and blood from his mouth. He slowly rose, pushing his chest and face up from the soil with both arms. He turned and sat on the ground and gazed into the eyes of his brothers. "You are my brothers and I am with you. I vow," Aspatha stated, remorsefully.

"Good!" shouted Dalphon to Aspatha. Dalphon motioned with his hand to his other brothers, "Pick up your brother." The other brothers helped Aspatha to his feet. They dusted him off and patted him on the back for making what they felt was the right decision.

*"Now! All of you go and round up the horses. Parmashta, Arisai, and I will come up with a plan to strike back at the palace. When you find the horses bring them back here to the house. We will get cleaned up and dressed for battle." stated Dalphon. Seven brothers went in different directions to recover their horses, while three brothers remained to devise a plan.*

*"What's our plan, Dalphon?" asked Arisai. Dalphon had a plan, but he was uncertain as to all the details.*

*"This is what we must do. We must first find someone who is willing to see fathers' decree take place. After that, we have to be able to arm all those who are willing to fight. Then we must strike immediately. The date must not change for the executions to take place. That's the key. But, by now the King must be altering the decree to save the Jews from execution."*

*"So we don't have much time," said Parmashta.*

*"No we don't. But, what I'm anticipating, is the decree has been in place for several days. So right now there are soldiers that are ready to take action against the Jews," said Dalphon.*

*"I see," said Arisai.*

*"All we have to do, is make sure the battles take place as planned," said Dalphon.*

*"But the King has 127 provinces. There is no way we can cover them all in just one day," said Parmashta.*

*"That's right, Parmashta. But neither can Mordecai, he has to send messengers to all the provinces to revoke the decree that's already in place," stated Dalphon.*

*"You're right, Dalphon. Well, do you know of anyone in the other provinces who would be willing to assist us?" asked Arisai.*

*"You bet I do!" exclaimed Dalphon.*

*"What? Who?" asked Arisai, surprised at the response.*

*"You don't think, I thought of all that just that quick, do you? Father didn't get where he was without help from friends. Aspatha was right. Father's plan to destroy the Jews also involved overthrowing the King. Father informed me of all his actions, being the oldest, he wanted me to complete his plan in*

*case something ever happened to him. He didn't brief me on the entire plan. But he did tell me to seek out a man named Bigota if something should happen to him," explained Dalphon.*

*"And why did father pick you? He could have picked Arisai or myself. We have the ability to lead men. What made you so special?" asked Parmashta.*

*"Nothing. He could have picked either one of us. I'm the oldest, so he went by maturity. He didn't want strife among his sons, especially with a task so great. So, father only told me of his plan."*

*"Ok, so father didn't want us to argue among ourselves, fine. He picked Dalphon, Parmashta, let it be. We all benefit no matter who knows the plan," said Arisai.*

*"Dalphon we knew father may have lied a few times to gain favor with the King, but was he really a ruthless person?" asked Parmashta.*

*"That's putting it mildly," said Dalphon.*

*"You mean father was a liar, and a fraud?" asked Arisai.*

*"Let's just say, father believed in being number one no matter what the cost," said Dalphon.*

*"Even if it meant discrediting his friends?" said Arisai.*

*"That's right, whatever the cost. You know what father's words were..." said Dalphon.*

*"There is no glory in being second best!" stated all three brothers in unison.*

*"And I never intend to be!" stated Dalphon.*

*"So with father gone, we finish his plan, we overthrow the palace and who is to be King? You?" asked Arisai.*

*"That's right. Me," said Dalphon, confidently.*

*"No wonder you were so strong on carrying out father's plan. So why were you so hard on Aspatha? You could have just told all of us what father's plan was," said Arisai.*

*"The other brothers are too easily swayed. If I had let Aspatha continue on his path of self righteousness, to forgive and forget everything and start over, we may have had a split group of brothers. Some of us may have sided with Aspatha and*

*some may have been with me. I couldn't take the chance of us being split. To make father's plan work, we all need to work together and be in agreement. So, when I knocked Aspatha to the ground, it was a show of force. The other brothers knew I was stronger. They all will now follow me, even Aspatha. Understand?" said Dalphon.*

*"Yeah, be on my side or get your teeth knocked out," said Arisai.*

*"That's right! We are sticking together on this. I promised father," said Dalphon.*

*"But father was wrong in what he did and you just want to be King," said Parmashta.*

*"Don't you start too with that right and wrong stuff. When we succeed, we will all live like Kings," said Dalphon.*

*"No I meant father was wrong in not letting all his sons know of his plans," said Parmashta.*

*"All of us wouldn't have understood. Some of us have to be led. That's the reason he only told me of his plan. We would have been fighting amongst ourselves to see who would take the throne. Trying to make decisions among us would have created chaos. We needed a leader. This way, father felt I was the strongest of us all. I know the plan and I have been designated by father to take the position of King. The plan has been set and all involved are aware that I am to be King."*

*"Let's go with father's plan, Parmashta. Living like Kings sounds good to me. I don't have to be a King to spend gold," said Arisai, "Who do we need to see to get some help in this endeavor?"*

*"There is a man called Bigota in the province of Randam. Once father changed the decree, he knew he would need help to ensure the proclamation was carried out. Bigota was one of several men who knew of father's plan. So he is our key contact. We can stay with him, I'm sure. Father and he were the best of friends," said Dalphon.*

*"Alright, now what?" asked Parmashta.*

"Now, we start helping our other brothers round up the horses," said Dalphon.

"Wait Dalphon, don't you feel now that the other brothers know you are in charge, that we should let them in on the real reason we are going against the palace?" asked Parmashta.

"Are you serious? Did you hear what Aspatha said? Avenging the deaths of our parents isn't reason enough to attack the palace. Do you honestly think if he knew father's plan that he would feel any differently than he does now? If anything, he would probably alert the King to our actions. No! Now would not be a good time to tell them. I will tell them when the appropriate time presents itself," said Dalphon.

"Very well," said Parmashta.

"Now, let's go find the horses," stated Dalphon. All three scattered in different directions to locate their horses.

# *Chapter 9*

## *The Executions*

*While the sons of Haman were occupied searching for their horses, Mordecai was working with the scribes in the palace drafting room preparing a new decree to rescind the previous one Haman had sent out. Mordecai knew time was short, but the message needed to be clear.*

*"Let me see what the King has told you to write," said Mordecai. Ischdi handed Mordecai the scroll.*

*Mordecai read silently. "People of my Kingdom, a few days ago, a decree was signed to kill the Jews in all the provinces. Those were not the words I wanted written. My confidant and second in command took it upon himself to alter my decree without my authorization. This, as you know, is a treasonous act. As of now, Haman is removed from office and will be hung at the gallows. The decree should have never been issued. Disregard the previous decree. The Jews are not to be harmed. It is not my desire that the Jews be killed. Mordecai is my new Chief of the Guards and he will enforce this decree." Sign King Ahasuerus.*

*"Ischdi, add three more lines repeating the words, do not kill the Jews, in bold letters, just above the King's signature. Then make as many copies for me as quickly as you can."*

*"I only have three other scribes besides myself. We are writing as fast as we can. But to add that statement will take just a little more time," said Ischdi.*

*"I understand, Ischdi, I just want that point to be made perfectly clear. The Jews are not to be harmed." Ischdi expressed sympathy for Mordecai's concern for loss of life.*

*"We will hurry Mordecai, we will hurry. When we have ten completed copies the way you have requested them, I will bring them to you," said Ischdi.*

116

"Good. I have 127 messengers standing by to ride. Do not delay."

"It shall be done," replied Ischdi. Mordecai turned to leave, but he felt troubled and saddened. He turned back toward Ischdi.

"Ischdi, I must do something now I don't want to do."

"And what is that Chief Mordecai?" asked Ischdi.

"As cruel as Haman has been to me, I do not wish to take his life."

"Mordecai, the decision to execute Haman is not for what he did to you, it's for what he did to the King. He deceived the King. That's punishment by death." Ischdi paused. He stared into Mordecai's eyes. Ischdi sympathized with Mordecai's emotions more and more. "Just give the order, you don't have to watch." Mordecai bowed his head in remorse for what must be done. He turned to walk out, but again he paused. He glanced back at Ischdi.

"Thanks Ischdi for your input. But I don't feel any better. But please hurry and get me as many decrees as you can. I'll be in the throne room with the King."

Mordecai left the room. Ischdi sat at his desk and started to write at an increased pace. He instructed the other scribes to do the same.

Moments later, Mordecai and the King met in the throne room. "My King, I reviewed the decree. It was fine. I just added a couple of lines," stated Mordecai.

"However you want it to read Mordecai, is fine with me."

"Thank you, Sire." Mordecai paused and stared at the King.

"What is it, Mordecai? You look troubled."

"May I speak freely?" asked Mordecai.

"Please do, you are now my second in command. I expect nothing but the truth. I want you to express your true feelings. But know this, I have the final word," said the King firmly.

"Yes, Sire."

"Well, what is it?" asked the King, curiously.

"Could we just exile Haman and his wife?" said Mordecai, saddened at the thought of execution.

"What! After he almost had all of your people killed? The decree was a threat of death against you and Esther. No! We can't exile them. Not only for what he has done to you, but, for what he has done to me!" The King lowered his voice. "A man like Haman who says he honors you in one breath and plots against you in another, seeks revenge. If he lives, he would try to carry out his plan. No, Mordecai, when Adak returns, have the executions take place immediately."

"Yes, Sire." At that moment Esther came into the throne room. She bowed to the King. Mordecai bowed to Esther.

"Breakfast is ready," Esther joyously pronounced. Both men appeared depressed.

"We are coming, Esther," said the King. The King looked at Mordecai. "Think about what I said."

"Yes, Sire." The King moved toward Esther and they started to walk down the corridor. Esther thought Mordecai would follow. When he did not, she paused and turned around. The King stood beside her.

"Aren't you coming, Uncle?"

"Noooo, my Queen, not right now. I'm not hungry. I have something I must do," regretfully spoken by Mordecai.

"Very well, Uncle, be sure and get something to eat. Remember how important breakfast is," smiled Esther. The King held out his arm. Esther laid her hand upon his and they strolled to the dining room. Mordecai made his way to the guard's quarters. The men were engaged in practicing hand-to-hand combat. They paused when they saw Mordecai enter the room.

"Who's next in charge after Adak?" asked Mordecai.

"I am Chief Mordecai," said a young man with a broad masculine chest, as he wiped sweat from his face.

"And who are you?" asked Mordecai.

"My name is Lud."

"Lud, when Adak gets back with Haman's wife, do not delay. Perform the executions immediately."

"I will inform Adak. It shall be done, Chief Mordecai," said Lud.

Mordecai walked away feeling depressed. He felt the same sorrow for Haman that he once felt for Hazor. Mordecai was headed back to the throne room when Ischdi spotted him in the corridor.

"Mordecai!" called Ischdi, waving papers in his hand. "Here's forty decrees." He handed Mordecai a small basket filled with scrolls.

"Thank you so much, Ischdi," Mordecai delightfully stated, "I will get these out right now." Mordecai made his way back to his office near the guard's quarters. He placed the King's seal on all the scrolls and immediately went to the guard's quarters. He saw Lud, this time engaged in sword fighting. "Lud!"

"Yes, Chief Mordecai." Lud placed his sword to his side and walked toward Mordecai.

"Take these scrolls and see to it that the messengers get them to the furthest provinces first. But, make sure two scrolls are posted in the town square of Shushan. Now hurry! I will be in the throne room with the King if you need me," stated Mordecai.

Lud responded quickly. He carried the scrolls to where the messengers were waiting and followed Mordecai's instructions. Lud was on his way back to the guards quarters when he spotted Adak and the other guards with Haman's wife coming down the corridor. They were walking toward the dungeons of the palace. "Adak!" called Lud.

"Take her to the dungeon with her husband and I will speak with Chief Mordecai to find out when the executions are to take place," said Adak to his guards.

Lud increased his pace to meet Adak coming down the corridor. Adak took his helmet off. Lud approached him.

"Adak, Chief Mordecai wants the executions to take place at once."

Danielle James

"Very well, prepare the prisoners and prepare the gallows. I will inform Chief Mordecai that we have arrived. Do you know where he is?" asked Adak.

"He said he would be in the throne room with the King," said Lud, as he went to prepare for the executions.

Adak went to the throne room to locate Mordecai. Mordecai was gazing through the window in deep thought about the executions. Adak knocked.

"Come in," said Mordecai.

"Chief Mordecai. Haman's wife is being placed in the dungeon as we speak."

"Thank you, Adak."

"Where's the King?" asked Adak.

"He's probably finishing breakfast with the Queen. I'm waiting on him to return. You know Adak, you didn't have to come and inform me that you had arrived. I told Lud what I wanted you to do."

"I know Chief Mordecai. But since my situation with Haman, I make sure the information I receive from anyone is correct before I execute."

"What do you mean?" asked Mordecai.

"A long time ago, when Hazor was Chief of Security, Haman and I were the two highest ranking soldiers in the King's Army. We were best friends, or so I thought. One day Haman told me Hazor wanted me to take one of the King's prize horses and deliver it to Prince Mali for a heroic act the prince had performed. I didn't really doubt Haman, but I did check with the Chief of Security in Randam to see if he was expecting a horse for his prince. Well, he said that he was and a stall was already prepared for the horse. When I got there, Prince Mali had no knowledge of what I was talking about. He contacted his Chief of Security and he said he had no knowledge that I was coming. The prince contacted King Ahasuerus. Well, neither the King nor Hazor had any knowledge of this situation either. It appeared as if I had taken it upon myself to give away one of the

120

King's finest horses. The King was furious and Hazor demoted me. I was devastated."

"So when Hazor was executed for treason, Haman was next in line for the position."

"Right," said Adak.

"Why didn't you try to get back at Haman?" asked Mordecai.

"Revenge isn't my nature. Over the course of my years, I've learned that the trap I lay for someone else, could be the trap I lay for myself. I just follow orders, be patient and wait my turn."

"I understand Adak. Well, what Lud told you was correct."

"Do you want to be at the executions?" asked Adak.

"No I don't. Neither does the King or the Queen."

"Very well, Chief Mordecai. It shall be done, now." Adak left the room.

Moments later, in the dungeon, Zeresh was tossed in beside her husband. "I'm sorry, Zeresh." He looked at her dress. "They didn't give you time to change your night gown?" Zeresh said nothing. She only wished she could put the noose around his neck. "How did our sons take it?" asked Haman, curiously. Zeresh did not reply. Haman moved closer to her and touched her shoulders. She quickly moved away from him to the other corner of the cell. Zeresh never said a word. She looked around for a place to rest. There was none. She bent down to brush dirt and rocks away for a small space to sit on the cold dungeon floor.

"So you aren't going to talk to me, now, huh? In our hour of need, you aren't going to even say, I told you so? Say something. Please. I am sooo sorry. What I did, I didn't think it would affect you. I never meant to hurt you," Haman stated, remorsefully.

With her arms wrapped around her legs, bent to her chest, Zeresh rested her chin upon her knees as she sat on the hard dusty dungeon floor. She just stared at the mildew on the walls and spider webs that stretched from one corner of the brick to *the other. She was extremely angry. She had been reduced from an enormous lovely home with several rooms to one small room with no chairs.*

*"Why don't you say something, darling?" She stared at Haman, her eyes filled with hatred and anger. But Zeresh said nothing and glanced down at the dungeon floor.*

*"At least we are leaving this life together," Haman stated sarcastically. Zeresh again, said nothing. She sat on the dirty dungeon floor, thinking of what she had told him about taking advantage of his authority.*

*At that moment, they heard the guards unlock the heavy wooden door. Haman moved back from the door. Zeresh leaped to her feet. Fear gripped their hearts. But Haman never expressed his fear and Zeresh never uttered a word. They knew their lives were about to end. They both said nothing. The guards escorted them out of the dungeon. The bright morning sun shined upon their faces, with her hand, Zeresh shielded her eyes from the glare of the sun. When she did, she caught a glimpse of the gallows in a short distance. A tower that stood almost forty feet in height with sturdy ropes hanging across a two by four of wood. Soon, Haman began the long climb of several steps to the hangman's noose and Zeresh slowly followed. With each grueling step she felt like it was an eternity. Finally, the last step and Adak was waiting there. He stood tall in full body armor, sword in sheath. The guards positioned them under a noose and tied their hands behind their backs.*

*"Place the noose around their necks and tighten it," spoke Adak to his guards. A slight moan came from Zeresh and a grunt from Haman when the guards pulled the noose tight around their necks. Haman was in thought of how to get out of this situation. Zeresh spoke not a word.*

*"Adak, old friend, my best friend. Don't let this happen. What would it take for you to let us go and you would never see us again?" asked Haman.*

"Haman you know me. I follow orders to the letter. Forgive me, old friend, my best friend, but you did this to yourself." Adak raised his hand to the guard.

"Adak wait! Don't hang my wife in her night gown," begged Haman.

"I wasn't aware you needed to be formally dressed to be hanged." Haman lowered his head. Zeresh closed her eyes and thought of all the riches she no longer possessed. Adak raised his hand to the guard again. A guard cloaked their faces. "Guard!" shouted Adak. The lever was pulled.

Unaware that their parents were dead, Haman sons had rounded up all the horses. They all stood dressed for battle in a circle waiting further instructions. They were ready to ride. "Do you think we could make it into town to stop the hanging?" asked Adalia.

"Be serious. We've been searching this land for hours looking for our horses. Do you think they are going to wait until we show up?" stated Arisai.

"Don't you want to know for sure?" said Adalia.

"No, I don't! If they survived, they will find us," said Parmashta.

"Enough!" shouted Dalphon. "What's done is done."

"Ok, we are ready to ride Dalphon. Where do we go from here?" said Aspatha.

"There is a province called Randam about forty miles from here. There, we will try to find a man named Bigota. He is a friend of our father. I'm sure he will put us up once we explain what has happened," said Dalphon.

"Ten of us?" asked Aspatha.

"Don't be so negative. Let's ride and find out," said Dalphon. They galloped swiftly down the dusty trails and low valleys of Shushan to reach their destination.

While the evening grew late, Mordecai had given the last of the scrolls to Adak to send out. Mordecai, Queen Esther, and the King all sat in the throne room. They discussed the decrees.

123

"*Do you think the messengers will make it in time?*" *said Esther.*

"*Esther we have a full day left. The furthest provinces are a. day away and that was where the first decrees were taken. They should arrive late tonight. I think we'll make it,*" *said Mordecai.*

"*Me too. Don't worry my Queen,*" *said the King.*

"*Don't lose faith, keep your beliefs strong, my Queen,*" *said Mordecai. At that moment, Adak knocked at the door.*

"*Come in,*" *said the King. Adak bowed to the King and Queen.*

"*The executions have been performed. Chief Mordecai the sons were told to move out of the house by tomorrow. If you wish, I can take a group of men there tomorrow and check?*"

"*That will not be necessary. I will not move from the palace until I am sure all 127 provinces have honored the decrees. And I want you to be on alert, Adak, in case I need you. If things don't go as planned, another strategy will have to be developed.*"

"*I will be in the guard's quarters,*" *said Adak.*

"*That's fine,*" *said Mordecai. Adak started to leave, when suddenly he had a thought. He turned around.*

"*Chief Mordecai, in speaking with the sons of Haman, they were not going to take this graciously. There may be a group of angry young men roaming the countryside with only one purpose in mind, to strike back at you and the Queen,*" *explained Adak.*

"*I will take that under consideration Adak. Thanks for the warning,*" *stated Mordecai. Adak bowed again to the King and Queen and left the room.*

"*What can ten angry boys do against a palace of armed guards?*" *asked Esther.*

"*It's not the boys so much Esther as the strength they would have in numbers?*" *said the King.*

"*I don't understand?*" *said Esther.*

"*What the King means my Queen, is the boys know they can't strike the palace without help. The problem comes when you don't know how much assistance they are going to get and from whom," said Mordecai.*

*"Yes, but we don't know if they are going to do anything," said Esther.*

*"That's true, my Lady. But it's best to be prepared," said Mordecai.*

*"But none would dare attack royalty?" said Esther.*

*"That's not true, Queen Esther. Remember the story I told you about Hazor?" said Mordecai.*

*"Oh yes, Uncle, I forgot. You're right."*

*"With your permission, Sire. I shall prepare our soldiers for battle just in case our decree is not honored."*

*"You have my permission," said the King. Mordecai bowed to the King and Queen and immediately left the room.*

*Esther had a feeling of concern that gleamed in her facial expression. The King, noting her discontentment, reached for her and she embraced him. "Don't let the threat of battle concern you my dear. Your uncle is a smart man. He won't let anything happen to you nor will I," said the King, boldly.*

*Meanwhile, the boys rode for hours to reach Randam. It was a small province with little market places of food and clothes for sale. When the boys approached the town, very few people were on the streets.*

*"I'm hungry and tired Dalphon. Where are we going to eat and sleep?" asked Adalia.*

*"Let's take care of business first. Those needs can wait. I want to find out where Bigota lives."*

*"But, I'm hungry too," said Aspatha.*

*"What did I just say?" Dalphon spoke angrily, "You sound like a bunch of babies!" The brothers hung their heads and leaned half off their horses from exhaustion and hunger.*

*"Let me ask someone where Bigota lives and we will ride there," said Dalphon. They saw a blacksmith shop at the end of town. They rode there.*

*"Excuse me," said Dalphon. "Do you know where I might find a man named Bigota or where he lives?" A tall muscular*

man was beating a horseshoe on a steel anvil, while sweat dripped from his brow. He raised his head to the voice that spoke to him.

"Yes, I know him well. He shoes his horses and the palace horses here. I can tell you where he lives."

"Where does he live?" asked Arisai.

"He lives several miles from here, heading north. Take you about an hour."

"Thank you, Mister," said Arisai.

"Let's ride brothers!" yelled Dalphon.

"Wait! Did you here what he just said. It's going to take about an hour. We've been riding for hours. I'm hungry, now! We haven't eaten anything all day. Can't we buy some fruit or bread from the marketplace?" asked Adalia. Dalphon rode closer to Adalia and slapped him across his cheek. He was so weak, he fell off his horse. Dalphon stared at his brother in the dirt. Then he looked into the faces of his other brothers.

"Anyone else hungry!" No one said a word. They all gazed at their big brother in command. Dalphon turned back to his little brother laying in the dirt, "Now get on your horse and let's ride!"

Aspatha got off his horse and helped his brother onto his. The other brothers started to ride off. Adalia rubbed his cheek gently, then climbed on his horse. They rode slowly to Bigota's house. They were weak and tired. Adalia and Aspatha rode side by side, just fast enough to catch up to their brothers.

"Aspatha we've been on these horses for hours. My stomach is hurting. Was I wrong for asking for some food before we ride on?" asked Adalia.

"No Adalia, I'm hungry too. But, Dalphon seems to be on a mission. So for now, we need to follow and be quiet. He is willing to hurt anyone that stands in his way."

Adalia rubbed his cheek and said no more. They rode in the hot afternoon sun for another hour. They finally reached Bigota's house. They all dismounted and walked toward the door of this enormous brick house. They knocked on the huge oak door.

"This house is almost as large as ours," said Adalia, not speaking to anyone in particular, as he glanced around the grounds. A servant came to the door. He was a middle-aged gentleman, some gray hair, slender in build.

"Yes. May I help you?"

"We are here to see Bigota," said Dalphon.

"One moment, please. I will announce you to my Master." The servant left to inform Bigota. He was relaxing with his wife in their huge elaborate living room.

"Master, there appears to be about ten young men at the door. They are extremely foul and filthy. Do you want me to get rid of them?"

"Ten young men?" thought Bigota, "No, show them in, Enal."

"Very well, Master." Enal led the young men into the living room.

Bigota stood about six feet in height. Not extremely muscular, but, medium in build. He had been speaking to his wife, Beka, a slender woman with black hair, brown eyes. They were discussing the decree that Bigota must honor tomorrow. When the boys entered, Beka stared at the young men. She rose from her plush chair and placed her glass of wine on the wooden oak table in front of her.

"If you will excuse me, my darling. I will let you conduct business," said Beka. She left the room.

"Ten of you?" said Bigota. "This can only mean you're Haman's sons? Am I right?"

"Yes, I'm Dalphon, the oldest. Father said to seek you out if anything ever went wrong. So here we are."

"So what happened?" asked Bigota.

"The guards came and got our mother this morning to hang her along with father," said Dalphon.

127

"Ohhhh, your mother too?" Bigota appeared saddened, but not surprised. "I guess his plan didn't work as well as he anticipated."

"That's right!" stated Aspatha, angrily. All the brothers turned in Aspatha's direction. Their facial expressions showed displeasure in his tone and words.

"Forgive me," said Bigota, observing their appearance. "You have traveled far to get here. I'm sure you are hungry and tired." Some of the brothers nodded. "Let my servant, Enal, show you to some rooms where you can get cleaned up. While you are changing clothes, I'll have the cooks prepare some extra food and plates at the dinner table."

"Yes, that would be wonderful!" shouted Adalia.

"Enal!" called Bigota.

"Yes, Master."

"Show these young men to the extra rooms upstairs where they can get cleaned up. Give them some of my clothes. Then have the cooks prepare some extra food for our guests and places at the table."

"At once master." Enal turned to the young men. "If you would follow me please." All the boys followed Enal to prepare for dinner. At that moment, Bigota's wife walked back in the living room.

"Bigota, those are the sons of Haman. Aren't they?" asked Beka.

"Yes Beka. They are."

"I overheard what happened to Haman. Don't go through with the plan. I'm afraid for your life too, my husband. You are all that I have."

"Perhaps you're right. It seemed to make perfectly good sense when Haman explained it to me."

"So now you can see how things can go wrong," cried Beka.

"I won't do it, Beka." Bigota reached for Beka and they embraced. She gazed into his eyes, lovingly.

"Good, you'll explain it to the boys," said Beka.

"*Yes, I will. They are joining us for dinner. I can tell them then.*"

"*Very well,*" said Beka. Bigota released her.

"*Enal!*" shouted Bigota. Enal came through the living room door.

"*Yes, Master.*"

"*My wife and I will be at the dinner table. Show the boys to the dining room when they come down.*"

"*Yes, Master.*" Enal bowed. Bigota and Beka went into the dining room. They waited only a few minutes before the boys arrived. Beka sat at one end of the table and Bigota at the other. The dining table was huge and laid with plenty of food and extra chairs. The boys began to slowly walk into the dining room.

"*Come in. Sit down. Take any chair you like,*" said Bigota. The boys quickly moved to a chair. Adalia was the first to sit down. Dalphon sat next to Bigota. Soon the boys were all seated. "*Boys, this is my wife, Beka.*" Bigota motioned his hand toward her at the other end of the table.

"*Ma'am,*" the boys stated in unison. Beka nodded her head in recognition to their response. But, they were trying to refrain from eagerly grabbing the food that was set before them.

"*If you would introduce yourselves, so we will know your names,*" said Bigota. Before anyone could say their name, Dalphon expressed his leadership.

"*I will introduce everybody,*" said Dalphon, he stood and went around the table, "*Sitting to my right is Parshandatha, Aspatha, Poratha, Adalia, Aridatha, Parmashta, Arisai, Aridai, Valjezatha, and I am Dalphon.*" He soon sat back down after the introductions.

"*Well boys go ahead and eat,*" said Bigota, "*But tell us Dalphon exactly what transpired with your father and the King.*"

"*The way we understand it, is our father altered the King's decree to exile the Jews. It so happens the Queen is a Jew.*" Bigota and Beka were surprised.

"*You mean the Queen is Jewish?*" asked Bigota, reaffirming what was just said.

129

"Yes, the King must have found out that father altered the decree to kill instead of exile the Jews and for that, he and mother were hung," said Dalphon. The other brothers stuffed their faces with food as Dalphon told the story. Beka listened.

"Well, I knew your father had altered the King's decree. His plan was not only to get rid of the Jews, but the King as well."

Aspatha raised his head from his plate when he heard what Bigota said. "What!" said Aspatha, "Why was father going to get rid of the King?"

"Well, your father's initial intent was just to get rid of Mordecai. But while he was speaking with the King, he thought it would be a good idea to get rid of all the Jews. But the King wouldn't sign a decree annihilating an entire race of people. Your father thought the King was a weak man. So, he decided to alter the decree without the King's knowledge. When he altered the decree to killing the Jews, your father needed help in Shushan for this to work, as the King's soldiers could not be apart of this massacre. So he had the word spread that he would pay a King's treasure to all that would assist in killing the Jews. After he had made that promise of paying gold for the lives of Jews, he felt that somehow the King might find out what he had done. He couldn't think of a good lie to tell the King, so, he thought it would be easier to get rid of the King as well." All the boys stopped eating. The story had become more intriguing.

"How was father going to get rid of the King?" asked Aspatha.

"Well in the midst of the battle between the Persians and the Jews, your father was going to slay the King and Queen blaming it on the Jew named Mordecai."

"But with father as Chief of the Guards, how was he going to say Mordecai did it?" said Arisai, "Father's job was to protect the King."

"He was going to send Mordecai an invitation to come and see the King. Since the King liked Mordecai, your father was going to think of a reason why Mordecai should come to the palace. Your father knew the King would sign an invitation for

*Mordecai to come. And on the day of Mordecai's visit, fights were going to break out in Shushan. Your father was going to use the battles as a distraction. The Jews were so upset over the decree, that Mordecai killed the King and the Queen."*

*All the brothers were in awe, except for Dalphon, Arisai, and Parmashta. "You mean father meant to kill the Jews and the King?" asked Aspatha.*

*"Without question. But, I see it backfired. Who could have guessed the Queen was Jewish," said Bigota.*

*"What was to become of Mordecai?" asked Aspatha, intense with the questioning.*

*"Your father was going to hang Mordecai in the town square for the murder of the King and Queen. It seemed like a perfectly good plan."*

*"Did father mention to you anything about a backup plan?" asked Dalphon.*

*"Indeed he did. He said the oldest was to take his place."*

*A surprised facial expression gripped all the boys, except for Parmashta and Arisai.*

*"What?" responded the other brothers in unison.*

*"You!" said Aspatha, "No wonder you were so adamant about striking back at the palace. It was never about father and mother. It's about Dalphon," stated Aspatha, angrily.*

*"Watch it little brother, or you'll find yourself eating dirt again." Dalphon turned to Bigota. "So, Bigota, are you going to help me become King?"*

*"King?" said Adalia. All the brothers were stunned.*

*"Yes, Adalia. My brothers, think of it. With me as King, we could do whatever we wanted to do." Dalphon stood from the table. "Shushan would be ours! All the provinces would be mine to rule! I could make you all a prince in your own province. Think of it!" said Dalphon with vigor. Dalphon realized all eyes were upon him. Beka shook her head gently, not to be noticed. Dalphon sat down. All the brothers began to smile and talk among themselves. Dalphon saw that his brothers were delighted at the aspect of him becoming King, except for*

*Aspatha and Valjezatha. They were obviously displeased with their oldest brother. But he knew they would follow, he just needed Bigota's approval. He glanced toward Bigota. He was smiling too. Now was Dalphon's opportunity to ensure Bigota would help with the plan. "Bigota, whatever my father promised you, you can still get. I will honor his words."*

*Beka stared at Bigota, trying to reflect in her facial expression what they had already discussed. Bigota gazed intensely at his wife for a brief moment.*

*"Ok, I'll do it," said Bigota. Beka rose from the table in anger. She glanced at Bigota and left the dining room, hurriedly. Everyone watched her leave.*

*"Did I say something wrong?" asked Dalphon.*

*"No, I did," responded Bigota in a low tone.*

*"Now, what was my father's plan?" asked Dalphon.*

*"Let's finish eating and I'll show you a map of how your father wanted to take over the provinces and the throne." After they finished dinner, all the brothers followed Bigota into his study room. "Here we are." Bigota pulled a large map from his fine oak wood cabinet. He spread the map on a huge wooden table for all the brothers to see. "Here is a map of all the provinces. Your father's plan was to have small battles against the Persians and the Jews to start in all 127 provinces. That decree is already in place." Bigota pointed to the different provinces on the map. "But fierce battles would be heavy in the provinces of Elishi, here, Gilgoen, here, Dibona, here, Heshnon, here and Randam, here. These battles were to be distractions. This would go on for two days. On the second day, your father was going to make his move on the King and Queen."*

*"Why did father need distractions?" asked Dalphon.*

*"If the King was concerned with battles among his people, he would not be alert to his second in charge plotting against him?"*

*"Why do we need battles to be fierce in these five provinces versus any of the other 122 provinces?" asked Parmashta.*

"*Right now the decree states all provinces will fight the Jews. The provinces I mention know your father as a friend. All the Chiefs of Security in the provinces I mentioned are aware of your father's plan. They have a stake in the destruction of the throne. They are more than ready to go into battle against the Jews,*" said Bigota.

"*But they don't know that father is dead,*" said Aspatha.

"*They don't need to know since Dalphon is taking his place,*" said Bigota.

At that moment there came a knock on the door. Bigota opened the door. "*Enal. What is it?*" asked Bigota.

"*A guard from the palace brought this to you. He said to give it to you right away.*" Enal handed Bigota the decree. "*The guard is waiting at the door for your response.*" Bigota opened the scroll. He read silently for a moment, then looked back at Enal.

"*Tell him not to wait, I will be at the palace as soon as I can.*"

"*Very well Sir, I will tell him.*" Enal left the study room.

All the brothers gathered about Bigota to read the decree. Bigota only read a few words aloud.

"*It says, the Jews are not to be harmed and Haman was hung for treason for altering the decree to kill the Jews,*" stated Bigota.

All of the brothers bowed their head, saddened at the news. They knew for sure that their father and mother were dead. Except for Dalphon, he was not phased by the news, he had become obsessed with becoming King.

"*Wow! They moved quicker than I'd thought,*" said Dalphon. He spoke quickly after hearing the news. Dalphon wanted to get his brothers minds back on the task at hand.

"*If this decree has reached all the provinces, then battles will not take place anywhere,*" said Arisai. "*And I want a province for myself!*"

"*Me too!*" said Adalia.

"*What are we going to do now?*" asked Parmashta.

133

"We don't need all the provinces anyway. What we'll do is ensure the battles take place in the provinces we have control over," said Bigota.

"Right. The King will still be occupied with the battles in five of his provinces," said Dalphon.

"Of course. While Mordecai takes his army to battle the five provinces, we can move in on the palace and kill the King and Queen," said Arisai.

"Now here's what must be done. Four of you must ride to the other four provinces and alert the Chief of Security that the plan is still in effect. You four will stay there to ensure the battles take place, while the others ride to Shushan and start battles there. And one of you will stay here, in Randam, with me," said Bigota.

"Four of us. Which four?" asked Aspatha.

"The four youngest," said Dalphon. "You, Aspatha, Adalia, Valjezatha, Aridatha and Parshandatha will stay here."

"Why the four of us? We don't know anything about combat or battles or fighting or anything like that. I've never picked up a sword other than to play with it," said Adalia.

"Adalia is right. The only ones well-trained in combat fighting are you, Dalphon, Arisai, and Parmashta. The rest of us are mediocre," said Aspatha.

"You won't have to know anything about swordsmanship. The men you will work with are well-trained in battle. They didn't become Chief of Security for nothing. You just follow them and they will take care of you," said Bigota.

"They won't know who we are or where we came from when we ride into town," said Adalia.

"I know, that's why I'm going to send a message along with you explaining who you are and that the plan is still in effect. They trust me. It will not be a problem. You will ride out at first light. It shouldn't take you more than a few hours to reach your province depending on how fast you ride. Once you get there, have the Chief of Security to start the battles late in the evening and continue into the next day. Scatter the battles all about the *province. That way, once the prince deploys his forces to stop the outbreaks, his army will be spread thin. He will send a message to the main palace that he doesn't have enough men to control the outbreaks around his province. Once the palace gets word of the uncontrollable outbreaks, Adak will deploy some of the King's army to assist in controlling the battles among the provinces. That's when we make our move. The other five brothers led by Dalphon will wait outside the palace watching for the King's army to leave. After they leave the palace to stop the outbreaks in the provinces, three of the five brothers will start small battles in the King's province of Shushan. Once the King hears of battles in his own province, he will deploy his remaining forces to stop these outbreaks. The palace will be left with just a handful of guards. The palace will be left virtually unprotected,"* explained Bigota with a smile.

*"And then what?"* asked Dalphon.

*"You and Arisai will go into the palace and slay the King and Queen,"* said Bigota.

*"How will we get in?"* asked Dalphon. *"You will be dressed like the palace guards. I can help in that department. I have all the equipment you will need."*

*"My father thought of this plan?"* asked Aspatha.

*"Actually, yes, with a little help from me and his other friends,"* said Bigota.

*"Since the Chiefs of the Guards are not in control of the palace soldiers in that province, just how do you intend to start these outbreaks? I mean the Chief of the Guard doesn't have his own army. Does he?"* asked Dalphon.

*"That's right."*

*You had no way of knowing that the decree sent out by our father would be rescinded by the King,"* said Parmashta.

*"Remember I told you about the men that had a stake in your father's plan? Well, your father promised a small fortune in gold to all those who would help eliminate the Jews. All the friends of your father as well as myself have a small group of*

men to assist us in our plan. Upon completion of the battles, they will be paid in gold for their labors," said Bigota.

"You and father anticipated the recession of the decree?" asked Dalphon.

"No, we were going to use these men to help us attack the palace. Because if the decree was in force, the soldiers of the provinces would have been carrying out the decree as signed by the King," said Bigota.

"I think I understand now. Since the decree is rescinded, you must use these group of men to carryout the battles instead of attacking the palace," said Dalphon.

"That's right. That's where you and your brothers come in, Dalphon. You will be outside the palace, waiting for your opportunity to enter," said Bigota.

"And where will you be Bigota?" asked Dalphon.

"I will be here, in Randam, creating small battles throughout this province."

"I thought you were coming with us?" said Dalphon, slightly nervous.

"Dalphon if you plan to be a King, you'd better start acting like it. Besides I couldn't leave your younger brother here to make sure battles take place in Randam. Could I?" Bigota firmly stated.

"And what about us, the young ones? You think father's friends are going to accept this new plan and listen to us? Someone they've never seen before," spoke Aspatha, reluctantly.

"I told you, I'm sending a message with you with my seal on it. That way they will know it is from me. The message will explain what has transpired and they are to listen to you. You all know the plan now. Do any of you have any other questions? Now is the time to ask," explained Bigota. All the brothers looked at each other, some still unsure of the detailed plan.

"Could you just clarify who is going where?" asked Adalia.

"Aspatha you can go to Gilgoen, Aridatha to Elishi, Valjezatha to Dibona, Parshandatha to Heshnon and Adalia will *be with me here in Randam since you are the least trained of all the brothers in combat," said Bigota.*

*Parshandatha was shocked. He was a medium build, even tempered, young man with black hair and brown eyes. "I thought I was going to stay here in Randam?"*

*"Since Adalia feels uncomfortable about all of this and the least experienced in swordsmaship, he can stay with me. I will train him. If that's ok with you Dalphon?" asked Bigota.*

*"That's fine," said Dalphon.*

*"Bigota, I have a question. You knew my father well. Why did he do all the things he did?" asked Aspatha.*

*"You're not on that subject again?" asked Dalphon, in disgust.*

*"I just want to know," said Aspatha.*

*"Aspatha, your father was an ambitious man. The more power and wealth he had the more he wanted. It didn't matter whom he had to step on or over to get where he wanted to be," said Bigota.*

*"And what about you? Is that the kind of man you are too?" asked Aspatha.*

*"Not really, I don't want power, I just want wealth," said Bigota.*

*"Enough questions!" Dalphon shouted to Aspatha, "We need to get some rest. It's been a long tiring day for all of us. Bigota may we spend the night here?" asked Dalphon.*

*"Of course, I'll have my servants prepare some rooms for you." Bigota left the study room to find Enal. The boys stood there in amazement of what had happened.*

*"I have never had to fight anybody before. I'm not sure I can do this," said Aspatha.*

*"Me too," said Adalia.*

*"You don't have to do anything. Just follow along and let the Chief of Security and his group of men do the killing. But, you just make sure that the battles breakout. Ok?" stated Dalphon.*

The youngest brothers nodded their heads. Aspatha just stared at his older brother shaking his head in disbelief that he wanted to be King.

"Go get some rest all of you. We have a busy day tomorrow," said Dalphon. The brothers were on their way out of the study room, when Bigota met them.

"Your rooms are being prepared. Some of you will have to double up and sleep on the floor. I only have eight spare rooms," said Bigota.

"Not a problem. Aspatha, Valjezatha, and Adalia will room together," said Dalphon.

"Why do we have to double up?" asked Adalia.

"You are the three youngest and I said so. Good enough!" Dalphon raised his hand to slap him. Adalia backed away.

"Good enough, Dalphon," said Adalia. Enal walked up at that time.

"The rooms are prepared, Master."

"Good. Well young men, get some rest and we will put our plan into action bright and early tomorrow morning."

"Good night," said all the brothers one at a time, walking up the stairwell to their rooms. The three youngest were the last to go into their room.

"You two can have the bed," said Valjezatha, the youngest of the two and the shortest in height of all the brothers. "I will take the floor."

"That's mighty nice of you brother," said Adalia. He jumped on the bed first. The bed and the room were huge. Aspatha sat on a small cushioned couch decorated with plush pillows across the room. Valjezatha just stood for a moment.

"You know, listening to Bigota's voice, he sounds an awful lot like the man I heard that night speaking with father about Adak in the study," said Aspatha.

"Are you sure?" asked Valjezatha.

"Noooo, not really," spoke Aspatha.

"That was a long time ago," said Adalia.

"*Perhaps you're right, Adalia.*" *Aspatha soon dismissed the thought.*

"*Aspatha,*" *said Valjezatha.* "*Listening to the plan downstairs I got the impression that our father was a ruthless person, no heart or feeling for anyone but himself.*"

"*I know. I never knew that he was that deceitful until that night I overheard him speaking to some man about discrediting Adak. That's when I knew,*" *said Aspatha.*

"*What are you two talking about. Our father loved us. Who cares about anybody else? He took care of his family,*" *said Adalia.*

"*At the expense of others hurt and pain,*" *said Aspatha.*

"*Why do you really care about a bunch of Jews anyway? We are about to become a prince in our own province. We are going to be able to do whatever we want, when we want. People will wait on us hand and foot. I can't wait!*" *said Adalia excited.*

"*Doesn't it bother you that innocent people are going to die because Dalphon wants to be King. It's not about the Jews anymore. Did you hear Dalphon talking at the dinner table? It's not even about mother and father, its about Dalphon,*" *said Aspatha.*

"*That's right,*" *added Valjezatha.* "*Aspatha why don't you try to talk to Dalphon again and see if you can change his mind about becoming King,*" *said Valjezatha.*

"*Don't be foolish!*" *said Adalia. He rose from laying on the bed. He stood before the two of them.* "*This is the opportunity of a lifetime. We will all be princes in our own province.*" *He paused.* "*How wonderful that sounds. Prince Adalia. I like the ring of that and you two aren't going to mess it up. The plan is already in motion. What could go wrong as long as we follow the plan?*"

"*I feel so bad about hurting innocent people. I just didn't realize father was so ruthless,*" *said Valjezatha.*

"*Stop whining Valjezatha. They aren't people, they're Jews. That's what father always said,*" *said Adalia.*

"*And just what does that mean?*" *said Valjezatha.*

139

Adalia thought for a moment. "I don't know. Father said they were arrogant and aggressive."

"Like us," said Valjezatha.

"Well, he never really explained why he didn't like Jews. Maybe it was that Jew, Mordecai that made father the way he was. Who cares, father didn't like them, so I don't like them. You don't want to be a prince. You're afraid and you're short. Nobody would follow you anyway. Prince Valjazetha, the short cowardly prince. Ha! Go to sleep and stop asking such absurd questions. Besides, we promised Dalphon we would avenge father and mother's death or don't you two remember that?" stated Adalia.

"I do Adalia, but not at the expense of other lives," said Valjezatha.

"I understand, Valjezatha. The problem is, that we know the difference between right and wrong. And now we have a choice to make," said Aspatha.

"We don't have a choice!" said Adalia, angrily, "We are going to follow Dalphon and that's, that. If you two don't stop talking this way, I'm going to tell Dalphon. He'll deal with you two."

"Adalia, is right, Valjazetha," stated Aspatha, tired of arguing with Adalia. "Dalphon would rather kill us than see us walk away. The plan is set. We can't go against our brother. Let's get some rest. I'm tired."

"Yeah, I'm tired too," said Valjezatha.

"Good! That's better," said Adalia. He sat back on the bed and laid his head upon the pillow. Valjezatha lay on the floor with only a pillow from the small couch that was in the room. Aspatha laid on the couch instead of in the huge bed with Adalia. All three were extremely exhausted from such a long day. Their eyes soon closed. They fell into a deep sleep. That night the entire house of Bigota was in a deep slumber.

Bigota rose before the sun set in the sky. He woke all the brothers by knocking on their doors. Bigota had stayed up late that night to prepare the messages before he went to bed.

"*Arise! Bigota shouted throughout the hall. The boy's rose rubbing their eyes. The morning had come too soon. However, Dalphon was the first into the hallway.*

"*Let's go, brothers!" shouted Dalphon, anxious to put the plan into action. The remaining brothers slowly exited their rooms making their way down the stairs.*

*Dalphon and Bigota were already waiting at the bottom of the steps.*

"*Come on boys!" shouted Bigota, "Let's go over our plan one more time to be absolutely sure everybody understands what is to take place and when." Bigota started to walk toward his study room. At that moment, Adalia called from atop the stairs, looking at Bigota.*

"*Don't we get breakfast first? It's not even light outside yet," said Adalia, yawning.*

"*If you don't stop thinking about your stomach and let's get on with the plan before I..." said Dalphon.*

"*Enough bickering!" interrupted Bigota, "Let's review this plan one more time. While we are in the study room, Adalia, I will have the cooks prepare some breakfast."*

"*Are you satisfied!" shouted Dalphon, staring at Adalia.*

"*Go ahead into the study, I'll be there shortly," said Bigota.*

*The boys made their way to the study room. Beka was coming down the stairs to speak with her husband.*

"*Beka!" said Bigota, surprised to see her. He met her half-way up the steps, "What are you doing up at this hour of the morning?" He kissed her cheek.*

"*I didn't know if you ever came to bed or not. When I awoke just now you were not there. I wanted to make one last attempt at saving your life."*

*Bigota appeared frustrated at the remark, but, he understood her feelings.*

"*Honey, the plan is full proof." Bigota touch her hand, lovingly. "Don't you want more than what we already have?" asked Bigota, humbly.*

141

"My darling, husband, we have plenty. We have wealth, we have a beautiful home and we have each other. Don't throw all that away for greed."

"You know, I could be the prince of this province. Guess what that would make you? A princess," Bigota said with a smile.

"I don't want to be a princess, Bigota." He released her hand. "I just want the husband I married without all the greed and deceit. Before you met Haman, you were always for law and order. He changed you. Now those boys are following in their father's footsteps and you are being dragged down the same path that Haman took. Don't you understand? Just like those boys, you are blinded by the money and the power that they think they can promise you." Bigota became furious from the words she spoke.

"I'm through talking to you woman! You've got it all wrong. What I'm doing, I'm doing for the both of us. You'll thank me when this is all over. Since you are up, have the cooks prepare some breakfast, while I finalize the plans with the boys."

"But..." Bigota interrupted.

"I don't want to hear another word from you, other than, "Yes, darling." Now go! And call us when breakfast is ready."

Beka stared at her husband. He walked toward the study room. She was fearful for his life. She knew in her heart the boys were going to follow in their father's path and their fate would be Bigota's fate too, if he followed them. Bigota entered the study room, the boys were finalizing the plan. "Ok young men, are we ready to do this?" said Bigota.

"Yes!" they all yelled. Except for Aspatha and Valjezatha, each with saddened faces.

"Alright, Aspatha when you reach Gilgoen today, find Motiss and give him this message. Bigota handed Aspatha the message. Aridatha in Elishi, you will find Balaam, Valjezatha in Dibona you find Bullstock, Adalia you stay with me, and Parshandatha, you find Ethan in Heshnon." Bigota handed messages to all that were traveling to different provinces. "Give *them that message once you find them. You will be working together. They will listen to you once they see my seal on your message and they are well trained in combat, so don't worry,"* Bigota stated with confidence.

*"That's easy for him to say. I have never had to fight anybody for anything,"* said Adalia, whispering to Valjezatha.

*"Dalphon you know what to do?"* asked Bigota.

*"Yes, Arisai, Parmashta, Aridai and Poratha and I are to ride to the palace and wait there until half of the King's army leaves the palace to put out battles in the five provinces. Once the soldiers have been gone for a few hours, Parmashta, Poratha and Aridai will start small battles throughout Shushan. The King will send the other half of his soldiers to stop those battles. Arisai and I will enter the palace disguised as guards and slay the King and Queen."*

*"Why do the two of you get to go into the palace and not us?"* asked Parmashta.

*"Father trained Arisai, Parmashta and myself in hand-to-hand combat for years, more than any of the others."* Dalphon looked at Bigota. *"He use to let us in the palace and practice with his guards at sword fighting and hand-to-hand combat as often as we wished. We are the best swordsmen among all of our brothers,"* said Dalphon.

*"Why didn't he train all of his sons the same way?"* asked Bigota.

*"I guess time didn't permit and father grew busier as more of his sons grew up. The time just wasn't there anymore. Plus, some of us had no interest in fighting,"* said Dalphon.

*"Well, no matter,"* said Bigota. *After breakfast we will get our armor and ride to our positions. Remember that the battles in the provinces are to start tonight. Any other questions, anybody?"* No one said a word. They glanced at each other as if everything was just fine.

*"Good, let's find out if breakfast is ready,"* said Bigota. He opened the door to the study just as Enal was about to knock.

143

"The Madame sent me to tell you breakfast is served," said Enal.

"Great! Let's eat," said Adalia. He raced passed his brothers to make it to the breakfast table first.

The rest of the boys quickly made their way to the dinning room. When the boys were seated at the table, Bigota waited a few moments for Beka to join them.

"Enal!" called Bigota.

"Yes, Master?"

"Where's my wife?"

"She said she would not be eating. She didn't have an appetite. Sir."

"Very well. Tell the servants to get the boy's horses ready to ride and to lay our weapons and armor in the living room." Enal nodded and left the room. Bigota turned to the boys. "Eat up young men. You have a long journey ahead."

The boys started eating. Bigota paused. He was in a daze. For the first time since their marriage Beka was not sitting across the table from him. He felt saddened that his wife felt the way she did. They had always discussed situations and came to an agreement. But Bigota felt strongly about this. Surely, once more wealth came their way, she would be happier. Bigota smiled and started to eat. They all ate until their bellies were full. Once they finished their breakfast, they prepared for battle.

"It's time. Let's go," announced Bigota. They followed Bigota into the living room. There were swords, shields and body armor laid uniformly for the boys on a huge table.

"We have our own swords," said Dalphon.

"You must use these swords. They have the royal emblem from the King's Palace engraved on them. All the guards that watch the King's Palace have these swords. This emblem is the same in every province. The King designed it himself," said Bigota. They immediately placed on the armor and chose the swords they wanted. While some of them played with their swords and stared at the length of the blades and admired the well designed body armor, Dalphon was dressed.

"Let's ride, brothers!" shouted Dalphon. Parmashta, Arisai, Aridai, and Poratha, were ready to ride. They followed Dalphon.

"Your horses await you out front," said Bigota. All the eldest brothers left.

"Aspatha, Valjezatha, Adalia, Parshandatha and Aridatha are you ready?" asked Bigota. Adalia was still playing with his sword and had only half his armor on. Aspatha and Valjezatha were hesitant in putting their armor on. Parshandatha and Aridatha were already finished.

"Is there a problem?" asked Bigota. He noticed Aspatha and Valjezatha were slowly putting on their gear.

"No, none," said Aspatha. Valjezatha and Aspatha immediately finished putting on their uniforms. Adalia was playing with his equipment and almost dressed.

"We are ready," spoke Valjezatha. He slid his sword into his sheath.

"You have your messages to give to the Chief of Security of your province?" asked Bigota.

"Yes," they spoke almost in unison.

"Good. Go to their homes. That is their headquarters for this plan, not the palace. They will be home by dark from their duties at the palace. Wait for them there. Just give them that message. Follow the map I drew on the back of the message to get you to your destination. It will get you straight to their homes. Good luck, young men."

"Good luck my brothers!" shouted Adalia. He stood by Bigota's side and watched his brothers leave through the front door.

"What do we do now?" asked Adalia, while he still fumbled around with the equipment on the table.

"We wait. It will take your brothers hours to reach their destinations. That's why the battles are to start late tonight. That should give all your brothers ample time to get to their province and meet with their point of contact to discuss the plan."

145

"Well I didn't have to put on my body armor right now."

"No you didn't."

"Look, Bigota. I want to be truthful with you," said Adalia. He started to pull off the body armor he had on.

"Please, go right ahead."

"I'm just sick about what happened to mother and father," Adalia spoke with little sympathy.

"I understand."

"But, I want to be rich and powerful as well. I want to rule my own Kingdom. I want to say what happens and what doesn't happen. I want to be a prince, just like Dalphon wants to be a King. With my own province, I don't have to listen to Dalphon and any of my other brothers. Do you understand what I mean?" asked Adalia.

"I think so. Well, when Dalphon becomes King, he said he would give you a province. You are going to have a chance tonight to fight for a province."

"No, no, no. You see, I have never had to fight for anything I wanted. The last time I had a sword in my hand, I was sparring with one of my brothers and I cut my chin. You see the scar?" Adalia pointed to his chin. "I haven't picked up a sword since. Everything I have ever gotten in life was given to me by my parents. I do not want to raise a sword against anybody."

"I said you didn't have to fight. You'll just be prepared to defend yourself with the sword and body armor. My men and I will do what is necessary."

"No, no, no. You don't understand. I don't want to see what must be done. I really don't care to come along. May I stay here with your wife?" asked Adalia. Bigota grew angry from his words.

"You sniveling little coward. No! You want a province! But you don't want to see or do what it takes to get one. Well, you are at least going to see what it takes to get one. No! I changed my mind, you are going to fight for it. Forget just coming along to observe. You understand me, boy!" shouted Bigota.

Adalia was startled by his sudden change in his tone of voice. He didn't say another word. He started to finish taking his armor off.

"No! Don't take it off. Put it back on. It might make you feel like a man." Adalia started to place his armor on again. "You and I are going to ride and see the band of men I hired. I was going alone, but you are going to be with me every step of the way." Adalia felt rejected.

"Why? Why do we have to go see them now, if we have hours to wait?" asked Adalia. "To let them know what our plan is?"

"That's right! The sooner they are informed, that's one less thing we have to do. Let's go."

They were on their way out the front door where their horses awaited, when Beka came to the stairwell. She watched the only man she ever loved, walk out of her life, perhaps forever.

Adalia and Bigota mounted their horses and rode down the dust trails of Randam. Adalia stared at Bigota with a look of uncertainty, afraid of what he might see or have to do.

"I'm curious. How many men did you pay to assist in this massacre?" asked Adalia.

"There are seven additional men, tough and rugged, per province. Unlike you, they are ready to fight," said Bigota aggressively.

"How much are you paying them?" asked Adalia while they rode slowly down the trail.

"We promised them a hand full of gold," said Bigota.

"A handful of gold? Is that all? For what you are asking, I would have wanted a King's fortune," said Adalia.

"When you have never had a hand full of gold, that is a King's fortune to you." Adalia said nothing more. They continued on their journey to see the group of men Bigota had hired to fight the Jews.

# Chapter 10

## *The Massacres*

*At the palace, Mordecai was briefing the King on the events of the day.*

*"Today is the day, Mordecai," said the King.*

*"Yes, Sire."*

*"I think if we make it through today, we might be in the clear."*

*"No, your Highness. I would say if three days pass and no incidents occur, then, we are in the clear," said Mordecai.*

*"If Adak was correct in his assumption about the boys, they would need time to prepare an attack. It's only been a day since they moved out of their home. Now, we must wait to see what, if anything develops."*

*"Are our soldiers prepared?" asked the King.*

*"They are ready as we speak your Highness," said Mordecai.*

*At that moment, Esther walked into the study room. She bowed to the King. Mordecai bowed to her. "My King and Uncle," said Esther, " I have an uneasy feeling about today."*

*"Don't worry, Esther," said Mordecai, "All the decrees should have reached their destinations by now. The prince of each province will enforce the decree. No harm should come to anyone."*

*"I hope you are right Uncle."*

*"Your uncle is right, Esther. You have nothing to fear," said the King.*

*Esther gazed into the King's eyes, "It's not me I'm worried about, it's the people of the Kingdom. The Jews in all the provinces must be fearful as well." Esther, with folded arms started to gaze out the window.*

*"Do not lose faith, Esther," said Mordecai. He watched her stare out of the window.*

Esther turned toward Mordecai. *"You're right as usual, Uncle."*

*"If the King permits, I will be in the guard's quarters double checking everything."*

*"You're excused, Mordecai."* Mordecai bowed to the King and Queen and left the room. While Esther gazed over the Kingdom, the King walked over to Esther and gently touched her shoulders.

*"There is nothing to fear my Queen."* The King whispered in her ear. He placed his arms around her waist and positioned his chin gently upon her shoulder. Esther gripped his arms tightly and laid her head against his cheek. They both watched over their Kingdom. Moments later, Mordecai arrived at the guard's quarters.

*"Adak,"* called Mordecai. Adak was practicing sword fighting with another guard.

*"Yes, Chief Mordecai,"* answered Adak. He stopped sparring and wiped the sweat from his brow with a towel he grabbed from a bench nearby.

*"You know Haman's sons better than anyone else. What do you think they would do?"* asked Mordecai.

*"I have met them all. But, I have talked to the eldest on many different occasions. He is very head strong and determined like his father. Once his mind is set on something, he is relentless in carrying it out. As far as the other brothers are concerned, they would just probably follow the eldest. If they try to launch some kind of an attack, I'm just not sure what it would be."*

*"Then I guess we will just let them strike first before we make a move,"* stated Mordecai. He left Adak and went back to his office. Mordecai looked at the map of the Kingdom. He looked at all entrances into the palace. All avenues of approach to the Kingdom he could cover, but the big question was who would be willing enough to help Haman sons and why? Mordecai walked to his window and watched the sunset for another evening.

Danielle James

When darkness fell upon all the provinces. Bigota was in the position to attack an unsuspecting Jewish family with Adalia and his seven men. Bigota knew by now that all the brothers should be in position to make their attacks.

"It's time," said a determined Bigota. He spoke to Adalia and the armed men with him. "We will work on the homes closest to the palace of the prince, like this one." He pointed to a house a few yards away.

"Why?" asked Adalia.

"We want the Prince to know that the decree isn't being honored so he will dispatch his soldiers. Once the soldiers are roaming the province close to town, we will hit the homes farthest from town. The prince will have to dispatch more soldiers. We will then hit randomly and once the prince feels he doesn't have enough men to control the incidents, he will send a messenger to the main palace for assistance. Remember? That's the plan we already discussed. Were you listening?" asked Bigota.

"I think I was listening to my stomach at the time. How about I wait at your house?" asked Adalia, sarcastically, with a smirk on his face.

"Not a chance." Bigota leaned from his horse and grabbed Adalia by the arm and pulled him closer. "If I have to drag you, I will. Your brothers aren't going to lay their lives on the line and you sit on your butt. Now let's go!" He released Adalia's arm, "That house in the distance appears peaceful enough. Draw your swords everyone and let's ride." Adalia did not draw his sword. Bigota looked at him. "You too, Adalia." Adalia reluctantly drew his sword from the sheath and held it to his side.

This same action was occurring in the other four provinces that Bigota had mapped out. Bigota and the seven hired individuals slew the family that lived there. Adalia watched. It sickened him to the point of throwing up. They came out of the house and mounted their horses quickly.

"Bigota, please, no more. I don't want to see anymore," said Adalia pleading, holding his stomach. Bigota ignored Adalia.

"There's another house, there, behind those trees, I can see the light. But this time let's leave the father alive to spread the word to the prince. Let's ride! And this time Adalia you will participate!" said Bigota. The seven men took off riding their horses swiftly through the trees. Adalia didn't move his horse. Bigota grabbed the reins and pulled Adalia along.

"Where did you get those men? They rode to the next house like they enjoyed what they were doing."

"They don't enjoy it. They just want the money. Now ride!" Bigota released his reins. They soon reach the house. The men were waiting near the house behind a cluster of trees for Bigota and Adalia to catch up. They all dismounted. When they approached the house ever so quietly, they peeked through the window. They could see a family of three at the dinner table. "Ready men," stated Bigota. Adalia had placed his sword back into his sheath.

Bigota whispered, "Adalia you lead the way." Adalia didn't move. He stood still beside the house with his sword in his sheath. Bigota turned to see him. Adalia was posed like a statue, too afraid to move. Bigota moved closer to Adalia's face. "You lead the way!" demanded Bigota in a low tone, not to arouse the unsuspecting family.

"Nooooo, I can't. I can't do this," replied Adalia softly.

One of the seven men whispered. "We are wasting time. Leave the boy. Let's get this over with."

"Go!" shouted Bigota to his men. The seven men raced toward the unsuspecting family. They burst through the front door, Bigota grabbed Adalia by the arm and dragged him into the house. A startled family, mother, father and daughter leaped from the dinner table. They moved, putting their backs against the wall. The father placed his body between the men and his family.

"Bigota, Chief of the Guards?" the father shouted, perplexed to the interruption upon his home, "What do you men want!" No one answered. The seven men raised their swords to the mother and daughter.

"No!" shouted Bigota, "Adalia will do it. Kill the mother!"

"Noooo!" shouted the father, surprised to here Bigota speak these words. The wife grabbed her husband's shoulders tightly. At that moment, three of the seven men pulled him away from her grip and held him captive by the arms. She reached for her husband, but Bigota pushed her back against the wall.

"Strike her!" screamed Bigota.

"I can't!" cried Adalia.

"Do it! And do it now! Do it!" Bigota shouted. Adalia drew his sword from his sheath. He placed both hands on the handle and raised it high above his head.

"Do it!" shouted Bigota.

"Nooooo!" shouted the husband. The mother fell to her knees. Tears were flowing from her cheeks. She placed both hands together, pleading for her life. Their daughter watched without a spoken word. Tears had wet her soft cheeks.

"Now! Boy!" shouted one of the seven men.

Adalia took a long look at the faces of this misfortunate family. Emotions of regret grew strong. Suddenly, the sword trembled in Adalia's hands and he dropped it to the floor. He bowed his head and teardrops fell from his eyes. Bigota pushed Adalia to the wall.

"I'll do it," said one of the seven men.

"Go ahead," said Bigota.

"No! Please stop! What is it that you want? Please don't hurt my family," shouted the father.

In one fatal blow, the mother fell across the floor in front of her daughter. The daughter didn't say a word. Tears flowed heavier from her eyes. She stared at her father puzzled to the action of these men. Bigota looked at the little girl. Adalia started to grab his stomach.

"*Noooo, not my daughter! Take my life, but, please spare my child,*" begged the father.

"*Spare the little girl, Bigota,*" said Adalia, firmly. Bigota looked at Adalia. Adalia gazed at the little girl's sad eyes. Adalia soon watched her baby blue eyes close as she fell limp to the floor from Bigota's sword. Adalia started to throw up. The father screamed hysterically. Bigota turned to the father and stuck him in the shoulder with his blade, while the three men still held him captive. The father dropped to his knees holding his shoulder.

"*Kill me too!*" shouted the father, tears flowed heavily, "*For you have killed all that I loved and lived for.*"

"*I need you alive to tell the prince we are not honoring the decree. We are going to slay as many Jews as we can!*"

"*But, you're the Chief of Security at the palace. Why are you doing this?*" cried the middle-aged man.

"*I hate Jews! Now go!*" shouted Bigota. Two of Bigota's men helped him to his feet. The man staggered and stumbled, but he moved quickly. Bigota watched the man race through the door. He reached his horse and rode like the wind to the palace of the prince. Bigota turned to see Adalia bent over at the waist holding his stomach and leaning against the wall.

"*How dare you even think you want to be a prince of a province, when you don't even have the stomach to fight for it!*" shouted Bigota.

Adalia raised his head while he still held his stomach. "*Killing innocent women and children, this is what you call a battle. This isn't a battle, this is a slaughter! These people aren't even armed and they have done nothing to deserve what we are doing to them.*" Tears fell from Adalia's eyes.

"*Oh, now you're a Jew lover, huh?*" asked Bigota.

"*Noooo, I just suddenly realized....*" He thought of what Aspatha and Valjezatha were talking about in the bedroom that night as he still leaned against the wall holding his stomach.

"*You suddenly realized what?*" asked Bigota.

153

*Danielle James*

"*Nothing!*" *screamed Adalia. He vomited again. Bigota appeared repulsed by Adalia lack of courage.*

"*Then get off the wall, pick up your sword and let's go!*" *shouted Bigota.*

"*I'm not going to anymore houses,*" *said Adalia.*

"*Don't worry, I can't bare looking at the sight of you throwing up everywhere we go. We are done for this night. Let's go!*" *shouted Bigota. The other seven men were already on their horses. Adalia and Bigota were the last to come from the house.*

"*We are heading home for now.*" *Bigota and Adalia climbed on their horses, "Let's ride!*" *stated Bigota.*

*They all rode back to Bigota's house. Adalia threw up all the way back to the house. They soon reached the front yard of Bigota's home. "You men can rest in the stables for now. I'll have my servants bring you some food and drink." The seven men rode their horses to the stables. Bigota turned to Adalia.*

"*Come on and get some rest.*" *They dismounted and walked toward the house. "You just aren't cut out for this I see." Bigota was still angry from Adalia's actions on the rampages. "Tomorrow night you can stay here. Just looking at you makes me sick." Disgusted, Bigota stared at Adalia and shook his head. They entered the house.*

"*Beka!*" *shouted Bigota.*

"*You called my husband?*" *Beka appeared from atop the stairs. Adalia stood in the doorway with his head bowed, holding his stomach, and covered with vomit. Bigota stood behind Adalia and pushed him slightly toward the stairwell.*

"*Help this boy get cleaned up.*" *While he held his stomach with one hand, he slowly climbed the stairs holding on to the wooden rail with the other. Beka met him half way. She wrapped her arms around his waist and assisted Adalia the rest of the way. Bigota went to the kitchen.*

"*Enal, see that some food is taken to the seven men in the stables and get me a glass of wine. I'll be in my study,*" *said Bigota.*

*The Story of Esther*

"At once Sir," replied Enal. Bigota went to his study room. Beka assisted Adalia to a bedroom. She helped him lie down.

"I'll get you some change of clothes and have the servants bring you some fresh water and clothe to wash with." Adalia grabbed her hand to hold her from leaving the room.

"Beka, it was awful." Beka kneeled beside the bed and he held her hand tightly. "I can't take it." Adalia started to cry. Beka held his hand close to her chest.

"I know, I know, Adalia. I asked Bigota not to do it. But, he wouldn't listen to me."

"Nothing seemed to phase him." Beka wiped tears away from his cheeks with the soft touch of her hands. "He slaughtered those people as if they didn't mean anything to him. As if they were animals," said Adalia.

"They didn't Adalia. They didn't mean anything to him," said Beka solemnly. Adalia continued to weep. Beka rose from her knees, she sat upon the bed and placed his head in her lap. She rubbed his forehead.

"Adalia before my husband met your father, he lived by the rules of the Kingdom. But one day he came home with a bag full of gold from your father. I asked him why did Haman give him a bag full of gold. He said, "Let's just say, I did him a favor." From that point on, he started doing more and more favors for any body who was willing to pay. His entire attitude changed as to what was right and wrong. I tried to talk to him about what he was doing, but the ease at which the gold came, meant more than my words. Now, wealth and more wealth is his objective." Beka looked down at Adalia. His eyes were closed. She smiled and held him while he slept.

Minutes later, the middle-aged father had reached the palace. He was bleeding from the shoulder and his clothes were covered with blood.

"Open the gates!" shouted the man short of breath, exhausted from his ride. The guards saw his bloody exterior and let him in. He rode through leaning off his horse. He dropped to the ground. The guards assisted him to his feet.

155

"I must see the prince at once! There's a band of men, led by the Chief of Security slaying Jews," said the man, almost unconscious. The guards immediately escorted him to the palace. Moments later, as anticipated, the prince quickly sent soldiers to patrol the area, thinking that a show of force would disband the group.

While the Prince's soldiers roamed the area closest to the palace, Bigota sat in his study, sipping wine. He was thinking of Adalia and Beka. Adalia was a sorry excuse for a young man and Beka misunderstood his intentions. She knew nothing of what it took to be wealthy and powerful. He decided to press on with the massacres. All the other provinces were under attack as planned, he couldn't alter his own plot because of a coward and a woman. Bigota took the last gulp of his wine and rose from his favorite chair. He immediately opened the door.

"Enal!" Bigota called, "Did you feed the men in the stables?"

"Yes, Sir."

"Then I'm gone. Tell Beka I will be back tomorrow night. By then the plan will be completed. Prince Mali may send guards to the house looking for me here. You know nothing of my position. I must finish what I have started to do. There will be no sleep for me this night."

"Yes sir."

"If we are successful Enal, by tomorrow night one of Haman's sons will be the King of Shushan and it will be safe for me to return home." Bigota glanced up toward the stairs. He then looked at Enal and slammed the door behind himself in disgust with Beka and Adalia. Bigota took his men from the stables and started again. This time, the rampages would start further from the palace. Adalia and Beka heard the door slam. She ran to the stairwell. She saw Enal.

"Enal, where has he gone?" asked Beka.

"He said something about finishing what he started," said Enal.

"*Thank you,*" *said Beka.* "*Oh, and Enal, bring up some fresh water and clothes for Adalia to change in. Get the clothes from Bigota's wardrobe.*"

"*At once, Madame.*"

*Beka made her way back to the bedroom. Adalia was standing beside the bed when she entered.*

"*He's gone again, isn't he? To do the same thing he has been doing all night,*" *said Adalia.*

"*Was that the plan?*" *asked Beka.*

"*Yes,*" *said Adalia remorsefully,* "*Beka, I'm tired. I'm going to lay back down if you don't mine?*"

"*Of course not. I'll leave you now. But Enal will be up shortly with some water and clean clothes for you to change.*"

"*Thank you.*" *Adalia, holding his head, sat down on the bed weary of the day's activities. He appeared almost faint. Beka raced to his side. She touched his shoulders delicately and laid his head gently upon the pillow and covered him with a warm blanket. Beka watched him. She brushed the hair back from his forehead and continued to do so until his eyes soon closed. She thought he was so young to be involved in such a tragedy.*

*While Adalia slept in the comfort of Beka's warm arms, massacres went on all night and into the next morning. Reports of deaths were flowing into the palaces from the provinces. The princes had dispatched all the soldiers they could to deter these massacres. When a show of force by soldiers did not deplete the rampages, the princes sent messengers to the main palace for immediate assistance.*

*By that afternoon, Mordecai had received word from all five provinces that Jews were dead by the hundreds and the soldiers were spread thin at the palaces from searching the provinces for the killers. Mordecai immediately summoned Adak.* "*Adak, gather 500 soldiers. We will send 100 soldiers to each province. I will pick four of our best-trained men to help me lead the battle against these murderers. You will stay here and guard the palace.*"

"*Why so many, Mordecai. That's almost half the King's army?*" asked Adak.

"*We don't know how many we are up against. Since they are random acts of violence, there could be several groups or just one. We don't know and I don't care. I just want to find the men responsible for the deaths of these innocent women and children!*" said Mordecai, angrily.

"*Very well, then let the five best trained soldiers lead the way into battle. I don't want you to die,*" said Adak.

"*Don't worry, I will take precautions. I will lead one-group and chose four good men to lead the other groups. And you don't leave this palace for anything. I want you here in case something happens. And under no circumstances, send out more soldiers from the palace, for anything. Understood?*"

"*Understood Chief Mordecai. I will guard the palace with my life,*" Adak stated with confidence.

"*Have the soldiers ready to go in a few minutes. I will inform the King of my actions.*"

*Adak quickly left the guard's quarters to gather the soldiers for battle. Mordecai was dressed in full body armor. Helmet in hand, he went to the King's throne room. He knocked.*

"*Come in,*" said the King.

"*My King and Queen.*" *Mordecai bowed upon entering the room.*

"*Mordecai, you are dressed for battle!*" *spoke the King, surprised at his attire.* "*What has happened?*"

"*Yes, Uncle what is it?*" asked Esther, concerned.

"*Our worse fears have come true. Hundreds of Jews have died while we slept last night. Massacres are taking place now, as we speak. I'm taking five hundred soldiers with me to prevent anymore bloodshed.*"

*Esther placed both of her hands to her cheeks. Tears started to form in her eyes.*

"*Hold on Mordecai. That's almost half the army. Have you thought this through? What is the situation?*" asked the King.

"*Five provinces have massacres in their villages. The princes have deployed all the soldiers they possibly can to prevent these out bursts of violence without breaching security at their palaces. They have asked for assistance from us to help control the outbreaks. I'm going now, to put an end to these tragedies. I'm leaving Adak behind to maintain security here.*"

"*Adak?*" *asked the King. He remembered the incident with his horse.*

"*Adak is a good man. He will not let you down. Trust me.*"

"*Very well, Mordecai. Adak will be in charge. So, some provinces aren't honoring my decree,*" *the King spoke solemnly,* "*Do you think this is what Adak meant by angry young men? Do you think this is the work of Haman's sons?*"

"*I don't know, your Majesty, but, I intend to find out,*" *Mordecai stated, confidently.*

"*If these massacres are the work of Haman's sons, before you go, have Adak to arm the Jews of Shushan and tell them to fight for their lives!*" *said the King,* "*Good luck.*"

"*It shall be done, my King.*"

"*Be careful, Uncle, I love you.*" *Esther walked toward him and gave him a lasting hug.*

"*Just pray for our safety,*" *said Mordecai. Mordecai bowed and quickly exited the room. Esther embraced the King still in tears.*

*Once Mordecai reached the front of the palace, Adak was waiting with an army of men.*

"*They are ready, Chief Mordecai,*" *said Adak. Mordecai surveyed the men and saw stern faces, shields and helmets on horses ready for battle.*

"*Adak,*" *called Mordecai. He mounted his horse placing his helmet upon his head.*

"*Yes, Chief Mordecai.*"

"*By the King's order, you are to arm the Jews of Shushan and tell them to fight for their lives, if battles should break out here. Do it at once!*"

"It shall be done," said Adak. Mordecai pulled on his horse's reins and raised his right hand, a motion for his men to follow him. The gates opened to let the soldiers out. Dalphon, Arisai, Poratha, Parmashta and Aridai were watching the town square a few hundred yards away from the palace under the concealment of some huge trees. They observed the soldiers leave the palace.

"It worked!" shouted Dalphon.

"The plan is working," said Arisai.

"Ok, go Parmashta, Poratha, and Aridai. Start the battles in Shushan," urged Dalphon. The three brothers eagerly raced to their horses and headed to the far end of the province to begin their rampage. Dalphon and Arisai started to practice sword fighting among themselves. They knew, only hours from that moment, that it would be time for them to make their move on the King and Queen.

While dusk started to fall upon Shushan, Adak prepared a group of men to take weapons to houses of the Jews. "Lud take eighty men and spread these wagons of weapons among the homes of the Jews throughout Shushan. Do it as quickly as you can."

"Adak, the new decree has been posted for a day. Do you suspect massacres to take place here, in Shushan?"

"I'm not sure if outbreaks will occur here, but we are just being precocious. If there is a plan to kill the Jews of Shushan, time is not on our side," said Adak.

"It shall be done immediately, Adak." Lud moved quickly.

While Adak and Lud were preparing weapons for distribution to the Jews, one of Haman's sons was on his way to the palace of Shushan from one of the five provinces. He was galloping straight for Mordecai and his army of men. "Mordecai," said Daka, one of his key soldiers, "There is a rider in a distance." Mordecai glanced to the North.

"You're right Daka." The young man soon approached the army. He slowed to a trot. Mordecai raised his right hand to *stop the pace of his men. The two soon met. They sat atop their horses a few yards apart.*

*"Who might you be young man?" asked Mordecai.*

*"I am the son of Haman," said the young rider. Mordecai was shocked. But he displayed an expressionless face.*

*"I am Mordecai. Where are you headed so fast?"*

*"To see you." Mordecai dismounted his horse slowly. The young man did the same. They both walked slowly to meet each other face to face. Daka and the rest of the soldiers stayed mounted and listened.*

*"Why are you coming to see me?" asked Mordecai, bewildered.*

*"I know what my father did and he was wrong. My oldest brother, Dalphon and the rest of my brothers are trying to finish what my father started."*

*"By killing the Jews?" questioned Mordecai.*

*"Yes, but that's not all. My brother wants to be King."*

*"Be King? How?" asked Mordecai.*

*"By drawing all the soldiers out to fight small battles in the provinces, the soldiers at the palaces would be spread thin. Since, you have come to help the provinces, your palace is spread thin too."*

*"But I have over 500 hundred soldiers still at the palace," stated Mordecai.*

*"They will soon be spread thin as massacres are taking place in Shushan probably as we speak."*

*"What!"*

*"We know the King will not tolerate disobedience in his town. He will send the remaining forces of his army to stop the outbreaks," said the young man.*

*Mordecai paused. He wondered. "You're probably right. Who is behind the massacres in the provinces?" asked Mordecai.*

*"It's a small group of nine men in each province. The leader is the Chief of Security of the palace in that province. One of my brothers is another, along with seven other men hired*

161

*for small amounts of gold to assist in the raids. Their meeting place is the house of the Chief of the Security."*

*"Very well, who's at the palace of Shushan?" questioned Mordecai.*

*"Five of my brothers are there. Dalphon and Arisai will go into the palace to attack the King and Queen. They were picked because of their fighting skills and would be best to defend against the guards. Once the remaining soldiers leave the palace to stop the battles in Shushan, that's when three of my brothers will start rampages in Shushan. Dalphon and Arisai will make their move on the palace at that time. Dalphon, my oldest brother is to be King and each brother is to receive a province of our choice." Mordecai thought for a few moments of how he was going to approach this situation.*

*"Daka, pick another man that you know can lead a battle charge. Give him forty men. One leader of forty men will go to each of the five different provinces. Go to the palace and inform the prince that you are there to help and let him know of our plan. You and his soldiers will work together to capture these murderers. Take guards to the house of the Chief of Security in each province. Secure his home. Wait out of sight until he arrives with his band of murderers. His house is their headquarters for these cutthroats. Then take them into custody and bring them back to the palace at once."*

*"Why would they return to their homes?" asked Daka. That would be the first place the prince would look for them."*

*"You're right Daka. Tell the Prince of each province to spread the word among the soldiers and throughout the province that the King and Queen have been murdered and Haman son is now the new King. If they think the King and Queen are dead and Dalphon is now King, they could be caught off guard thinking it's only a matter of time before the prince of each province is dethroned. Their work would be done and it would be safe to return home knowing that one of Haman's sons will soon be the new prince."*

*"If we encounter resistance from these men?" asked Daka.*

162

"*Do what you must do to protect yourselves. I'm heading back to Shushan to prevent anymore bloodshed. Now, go swiftly.*"

*Daka did as Mordecai instructed. They rode immediately to capture these men. Mordecai watched them gallop off. He then turned and looked at the young man. "You will come with me," said Mordecai, "Mount your horse." He mounted his horse and so did Mordecai. Mordecai raced back to Shushan with the rest of his army. The young man rode proudly by his side.*

*Just as Mordecai was returning to the palace, Lud had already started to distribute weapons to the Jews of Shushan. He worked from within the city to the out skirts of the city. The word had spread of Jews being slaughter in neighboring provinces. No Jewish person refused arms.*

*The three brothers were starting on the outskirts of town first with their slaughters and working their way back into the city. They had been riding for hours through valleys and small towns, trotting along.*

"*You know, we should not be riding so slow. We need to hurry and get this done.*" *said Aridai, mild tempered, easy to get along. He had a slender build, long black hair and sideburns.*

"*I've been thinking. I really don't want to do this. We have never killed anybody or anything and I don't want to start now. Besides it will take us all night to go from house to house to house,*" *said Poratha. He had a medium build and a masculine chest, but, quick tempered and unwilling to sacrifice his life for a cause.*

"*Don't you want the wealth and the power? Remember, you can have your own province,*" *said Aridai.*

"*Yeah, but I don't want to die trying to get it. Father didn't tell us. He told Dalphon. Father didn't teach us how to fight with swords. The closest I got to fighting with a sword was playing with Adalia and I cut his chin. So we didn't sword fight anymore after that incident. He taught Dalphon, Arisai and you, Parmashta. You three fought hand-to-hand combat with the guards at the palace for months. So he meant for Dalphon to do*

163

*this without our help. Somehow we all got dragged into it," said
Poratha.*

*"What are you afraid of?" asked Parmashta.*

*"You were well-trained in combat. You know very well how
to protect yourself. But, for us," he pointed to himself and his
other brother, "If we encounter heavy fighting from the Jews, we
could be killed," said Poratha.*

*"Why do you say that?" asked Parmashta.*

*"By now, surely the word has spread about the massacres of
the Jews in the other provinces. This isn't like a Jewish wedding
where the rest of the town could be told the next day if they
didn't come to the wedding. These people are getting slaughter.
They are all probably just waiting behind their doors for some
unsuspecting fools like us, to burst into their homes."*

*"The Jews are pleasant people, they aren't really fighters,"
said Aridai.*

*"Anybody is a fighter when their life is threatened," said
Poratha. "If we burst into a home, they may not have swords,
but they have knives, and sticks and whatever else they need to
protect themselves. And BAM! We walk right into an ambush.
You might survive, but the rest of us may lose our lives and I'm
not willing to take that risk. I don't know about you, my
brothers, but I want to be able to spend gold and rule a province.
I can't do that if I'm dead."*

*"Well you're right about one thing, I don't want to die trying,
to get a province either," said Parmashta.*

*"Yes, you're right. If we were dead, it would be hard to
enjoy our wealth. So what do you propose, Poratha?" asked
Aridai.*

*"I don't know," said Poratha. They pondered for a few
moments, when suddenly they had an idea.*

*"I've got it! Let's do like Bigota," said Parmashta.*

*"What's that?" asked Aridai.*

*"Well Bigota was paying for the services of some men to
help make the raids on the Jews," said Parmashta.*

*"So?" said Aridai.*

"So, we can do the same thing," said Parmashta.

"How do you think we can pay people for helping us eliminate the Jews?" asked Poratha. He brushed his dark brown hair back from his eyes, while he thought.

"When Dalphon becomes King we will have all the gold we need to pay people. We just offer them a King's treasure and watch them do the work, instead of us," said Parmashta.

"That just might work," said Aridai, considering the idea.

"Well, I like it. What are we waiting for? Let's head back toward town. Then we can join Dalphon in overthrowing the palace," said Poratha.

All three men agreed not to bloody their hands and risk their lives. They made a speedy retreat back to Shushan. By this time, Lud had already reached the outskirts of town distributing weapons to all the Jews. The Jews of Shushan were now armed with weapons, ready to defend themselves.

Now that the Jews were armed, Adak was informing all the palace guards to be on alert for anyone or anything suspicious. He posted extra guards on the palace walls. He lined the corridors with several guards instead of the usual two. The King noticed the extra security in the corridors.

"Adak, do you think it necessary to post these many guards in the palace?" asked the King.

"Your Majesty, your safety and the Queen's is my responsibility when Mordecai is not here. I deem it necessary, until the palace is back to full staff."

"Very well, carry on," said the King, he started to walk back toward his study.

"My King," called Adak, curious about the fight over the Jews. The King turned around to face Adak. "If all of this is just about the Jews----And I'm not trying to offend you, Sire. But, why not save yourself the trouble and denounce the Queen?"

"Denounce my wife. Adak, I love her. I couldn't be more happier than I am right this very moment. You see, I wanted a beautiful woman and I didn't care if she was Persian, Jewish,

165

*Hebrew or any other nationality. I just happened to be lucky enough to get beauty along with personality and heart. If I had placed limits or stipulations on the bride I wanted, I would have never found Esther."*

*"I see."*

*"Adak, I don't care who you are as long as you don't disobey my rules or attack my Kingdom. You can believe in anything you want. All I am concerned about is receiving the honor and respect a King deserves."*

*"Understood, my King," said Adak. The King left Adak and returned to his study room. Esther was in the King's study room peering through the window.*

*"Esther don't worry. Adak is doubling security just for our safety," said the King.*

*"You don't think they can get in the palace, do you, my husband?" Esther asked, sounding a little nervous.*

*"No, my darling." He reached to embrace her. "No harm shall come to you as long as there is breathe in my body." The King kissed her on the forehead. "Why don't you go to your bedroom and get some rest."*

*"Alright." The King released her. She bowed and left the room. Adak saw the Queen come from the King's study room.*

*"My Queen!" called Adak, with two guards standing behind him. The Queen approached Adak. He bowed to her.*

*"With the Queen's permission, these two guards will be posted outside your door until further notice."*

*The King was on his way from his study and overheard what Adak had said. "Good idea!" shouted the King. Esther turned to look at the King with concerned eyes. "Walk her to her room, now, please." Adak motioned to the guards to escort the Queen to her room. Esther walked slowly down the corridor. The guards followed her. Once Esther was in her room Obtisse was there cleaning.*

*"My Queen, you look frightened. What is wrong?" asked Obtisse.*

"Obtisse we must pray." Esther kneeled down beside her bed and began to pray. Obtisse kneeled beside her and closed her eyes. Esther began to pray.

"Dear God in heaven, tragedy has fallen all around us. Place your watchful eyes upon us and guide my Uncle Mordecai to end this bloodshed throughout the provinces. In God's almighty name, I pray, Amen.

The King had waited until Esther was out of sight.

"Alright, Adak, you know something, spit it out!" said the King.

"No, Sire. I don't," innocently spoken by Adak.

"Why all the extra security?"

"Sire you weren't at their house when I told those young men that their mother was going to hang with their father for treason. I know Dalphon. He has his father's determination and spirit. He will not quit until he has revenge for what was done to his father and mother."

"So you believe, somehow, he can make it into the palace?" asked the King.

"I don't know, Sire. I just want to be ready in case he does."

"Very well, Adak, I guess I was wrong about you. I'll be in my study if you need me," said the King. Adak bowed and the King left for his study room. Adak continued on his rounds of the palace. When he had finished he went back to the guard's quarters. All was quiet for a few hours until someone called his name.

"Adak! Adak!" cried one of the guards with his sword and shield in his hand. "I just came from the palace walls."

"What is it?" asked Adak.

"Skirmishes have broken out in the town. You can see the Jews and Persians fighting in the town square!" the guard spoke, excitedly.

"How can that be?" Our decree was posted first! Who would dare defy the King's..." Adak paused, he remembered what he had told the King hours ago about Dalphon.

167

"Go back to the gates. Let no one in and I mean no one. Understood? I'll be there shortly. I must inform the King. Now go!" said Adak. The guard raced back to inform the other guards of the orders he had just received. Adak made his way to the King's study room. He knocked.

"Come in," stated the King.

"My King! Fighting has broken out in the town square among the Jews and the Persians," stated Adak, execited.

"What! This means that my decree is not being honored in my own province. I don't care if it's Haman's sons or not! I will not tolerate this disobedience among my people!" shouted the King. "Do you know if these outbreaks are just in the town square or are they all over Shushan?"

"I don't know, Sire."

"Then take the rest of the soldiers and scan Shushan for violent acts and stop them! Whoever they are. Bring them in so that justice can be done! I'm tired of people disobeying my rules. Now go!" shouted the King.

"Forgive me, Sire. But Shushan is a huge territory to cover, sending the rest of the army to fight battles would leave the palace with only a handful of guards for security. Do you think this is wise?" asked Adak.

"You've doubled security, Adak. How could anyone possibly get in? People are dying in the streets and probably in their own homes. We have to stop this bloodshed, Adak, and stop it now!" demanded the King, firmly.

"As you wish, Sire. But I will have a guard bring your sword and armor."

"Do that. I will be here, in my study."

## Chapter 11

## *Attempted Murders*

*While Adak prepared the last of the King's army for battle, the three brothers had returned to their original hiding place. "What are you all doing back here? You are supposed to be on a killing rampage throughout Shushan!" exclaimed Dalphon. Arisai was surprised to see them too.*

*"Look at the town square," said Parmashta.*

*"We noticed," said Arisai.*

*"Well, we started that feud out there and fighting should be breaking out all over Shushan about now," said Parmashta.*

*"What did you do to cause such an outbreak?" asked Dalphon.*

*"We promised gold to all Persians who would help us eliminate the Jews," said Parmashta.*

*"What?" said Dalphon, stunned from the remark.*

*"It's working. Look!" said Parmashta. He pointed to people fighting in the square.*

*"You'll pay the Persians, won't you?" asked Poratha.*

*"I'm not paying anybody anything. If they come to me looking for gold, they'll have a choice, their life or no life. I didn't tell you to promise anybody anything! You were just trying to get out of your responsibilities," Dalphon said angrily.*

*The brother's facial expression reflected anger and disgust with Dalphon.*

*"You just want somebody to die on your behalf! What we did was clever. I don't know why you don't think so?" said Poratha, in an aggressive tone.*

*"Are you arguing with me!" shouted Dalphon. He walked toward Poratha with his fist clinched.*

*"Look!" shouted Arisai. "The soldiers are leaving the palace." The brothers could hear Adak giving orders coming through the gates.*

169

Danielle James

"Soldiers disperse and stop the fighting. The rest of you come with me," said Adak. Some soldiers dismounted, drew their swords and charged the mass of angry bodies clanging metal to metal in the heat of battle. Dalphon paused. He turned from Poratha to observe the soldiers.

"Great!" shouted Dalphon. "That's Adak leading the group of soldiers. Now it's time to make our move. When we get inside the palace gates you three stand guard on the palace walls to make sure there are no surprises."

"Why do we have to stand guard? Why can't we go in the palace with you?" asked Parmashta.

"I don't want any more bright ideas from you or your other brothers. Arisai and I will handle the King and Queen. Do I make myself clear?" shouted Dalphon.

"What about the guards?" asked Parmashta, "You could use my help. I'm an excellent swordsman. I've even beat you sometimes, Dalphon."

"We can handle the palace guards by ourselves. Just do as I ask and guard the wall. Warn us at the first sign of danger," said Dalphon, "I just don't want any mistakes." Poratha felt rejected along with Aridai and Parmashta.

"Now let's move!" shouted Dalphon. The brothers raced toward the town square from behind their concealment of trees. They were all dressed like palace guards. They intermingled with the crowd as the soldiers were trying to breakup the fights in the square. When the last horse rode through the gates, all five brothers had made their way on to the palace grounds, unnoticed. "Act like guards you three. Act like you belong on the wall. Now go!" demanded Dalphon. The three brothers climbed the wall to stand as sentinels. Dalphon and Arisai watched their brothers move into position. "Let's go, Arisai."

As Dalphon and Arisai headed toward the palace, Lud was returning from his mission of distributing weapons to the Jews. Adak met him a few hundred yards from the town square.

"Lud!" hailed Adak. Lud rode with his eighty men to quickly meet with Adak. Lud could see the town square.

170

*"Adak what has happened?" asked Lud.*

*"Fights have started here. I left a few soldiers behind to stop the fights in the town square. Now I'm going to make sure battles haven't broken out in Shushan. Did you see any outbreaks at any houses or villages on your way back to town?" asked Adak.*

*"No, but we came from the outskirts of Shushan. We didn't come back the way we went. So I'm not sure if battles have broken out among the citizens."*

*"Very well, I want you to take my soldiers. They are well rested and ready for battle. Station them throughout Shushan. They have been informed as to what to do. You make it happen. I'll take the eighty men that you have back with me into the palace to ensure the safety of the King and Queen."*

*Lud did as Adak instructed. Adak was headed back to the palace, when off in a distance he spotted a group of horsemen. He rode quickly in their direction. They soon approached each other. "Mordecai!" shouted Adak.*

*"Adak! What are you doing out here with this small band of men? I gave you explicit instructions not to leave the palace. To guard the King and Queen with your life, if need be. Why have you disobeyed my orders?" stated Mordecai firmly.*

*"It's the King's order that I send the remaining soldiers to stop fighting in Shushan."*

*"Battles in Shushan have broken out?" asked Mordecai.*

*"Yes, they are fighting in the town square as we speak," said Adak.*

*"How long has this been going on?" asked Mordecai.*

*"Not long. It started a little while ago. Lud has armed all the Jews in Shushan and he has 400 hundred soldiers searching the province right now for disrupters."*

*"Ok," said Mordecai, "Let's ride." At that moment, Adak noticed the young man riding with Mordecai. As they rode along, Adak was curious about the new rider. His face was familiar.*

171

"Mordecai, I know that young man. He's one of Haman's sons," said Adak.

"You're right, I'll explain later. Right now we have to clean up Shushan."

When they approached the town square, Mordecai saw fighting in every corner of the town and all over the square. He immediately surrounded the square with his army of 300 soldiers. Soon his army was in position to strike the unsuspecting crowd. "Lay down your weapons citizens of Shushan or die where you stand!" shouted Mordecai.

All fighting ceased. The towns people looked around. Soldiers were everywhere with swords drawn, ready to fight. The three brothers on the wall saw the soldiers ride back into the town square and completely diminish the violence. "Look, Aridai and Parmashta," said Poratha; "It's Adak and Mordecai together. Something has gone wrong." They could not see their brother. He was concealed in between other soldiers.

"I see," said Aridai.

"We must warn Dalphon and Arisai," said Parmashta.

"You're right. Let's go," said Aridai. They quickly climbed down from the wall to alert their brothers of Mordecai and Adak's return.

"Hold on," said Poratha, when they all reached the ground.

"What's wrong?" asked Parmashta. Both brothers turned to see why Poratha had stopped running.

"Mordecai and Adak are coming in here soon. We need to get out of here," warned Poratha.

"And leave our brothers behind?" asked Parmashta.

"The soldiers will be surrounding the palace soon. We'll be trapped if we don't leave now. If we stay, we will surely be caught," said Poratha.

"And leave your brothers in there to die," said Parmashta.

"We are all going to die if we get caught. What do you say, Aridai? Do you want to go in the palace and warn them or save yourself?"

172

*"I'm going in. My brothers are in there and we just can't turn our backs on them. What if that were you in the palace, would you want us to leave you? You go on if you want to, we'll understand,"* said Aridai. Poratha thought for a moment.

*"Father said if the odds are stacked against you, retreat evaluate and try again later."*

*"He didn't mean against your own family,"* said Aridai.

*"Ohhhh alright! Make me feel like the bad one. Let's go,"* reluctantly stated by Poratha. *"We are going to die."* All three moved in the direction of the palace, one behind the other. They raced toward the entrance, they could hear Mordecai plainly laying down the rules to the people of the town.

*"Citizens of Shushan, what you have done is wrong. The King issued a decree and you have not honored it. Disperse and go home or die for treason where you stand. It's your choice. Go home and spread the word that all that continue to fight, will hang, when caught. The soldiers will be enforcing this throughout Shushan. Now go!"* The people scattered immediately. The square was soon emptied.

*"Mordecai,"* said Adak.

*"Yes."*

*"Haman's sons are probably behind this mess."*

*"I know, Adak. They are. This young man has done me justice. I now know what Dalphon's plan is. But I don't know what he looks like."*

*"I do,"* volunteered Adak.

*"Mordecai we must get in the palace at once. By now my brothers are surely in position for an attack on the Queen and King,"* warned the young man. Mordecai knew the young man was right.

*"Adak you take these soldiers and surround the outer and inner perimeter of the palace. Let no one in or out. No one!"* ordered Mordecai.

*"But you don't know what his brothers look like,"* said Adak.

173

"That's why I'm taking him with me." Mordecai pointed to the young man. "He and I will go in through the rear of the palace. After you complete my orders, you come in the front of the palace and secure the rooms and hallways as you enter. Now go!" Adak moved out quickly.

"Let's go young man," said Mordecai. They rode to the rear entrance of the palace. When they entered through the kitchen, they heard swords clanging and furniture being knocked over. "You stay here." Mordecai drew his sword. "I'm going to see whose fighting." When Mordecai opened the door, he saw King Ahasureus engaged in battle with one of Haman's sons. Mordecai immediately joined the battle. He lunged at the young man.

"Noooo!" shouted the King, sword fighting with the young man, "I saw two of them. The other one must have gone for the Queen. Go check on Esther! Hurry! I have this one under control." The King jabbed at the young man.

Mordecai raced toward Esther's room, he saw guards unconscious, perhaps dead, bleeding on the floor from sword wounds. These two men had left a path of blood throughout the palace corridor.

Mordecai increased his pace toward Esther's room. Dalphon was already there.

"My Queen what I do now, I do for my mother and father that you had hanged."

"Young man..." said the Queen.

"My name is Dalphon, soon to be King of this province." He pointed his sword at her. Obtisse stood against the wall short of breath from fear that gripped her heart of what was about to happen. The Queen stood next to her bed. Dalphon was still at the door.

"I had no desire to hang your father or mother. They chose the way they lived. Your father knew the consequences of his actions. If you put down the sword, I promise no harm will come to you," said Queen Esther.

174

"You Jews are all alike. Even in the face of death you're trying to give me orders. My father said you Jews were arrogant," said Dalphon. "Enough talk. It's time to die!" Dalphon lunged at the Queen with his sword. Obtisse threw her body in front of the Queen. Dalphon's sword pierced Obtisse's shoulder. The Queen caught Obtisse in her arms. Dalphon withdrew his sword from her shoulder.

"Obtisse!" cried the Queen. Obtisse fell almost lifeless in her arms. Dalphon was unphased by Obtisse's theatrics.

"No matter, she only prolonged your life for a few moments my Queen," said Dalphon.

Soon Mordecai saw the two guards that were posted outside Esther's door lying upon the floor. At that moment, Dalphon started to lung again. Mordecai burst through the door with his sword drawn. Startled by the noise, Dalphon whirled around. Mordecai stood firm and forceful, with his sword drawn, he pointed it at Dalphon. "I'm the one you want. I'm Mordecai. Fight me if you must blame someone for your parent's death."

Dalphon turned to Esther. "I'll be back for you. Now you can watch your uncle die."

Esther pulled Obtisse back from the middle of the floor. The two men began to fight.

"Ok Jew! Let's see what you are made of." Dalphon pointed his sword at Mordecai and swung. Mordecai countered and swung back at Dalphon. Mordecai made slashing motions at Dalphon. He dodged them and countered with his sword, jabbing at Mordecai.

As the battle raged with Mordecai and Dalphon, Adak had completed his order and entered the front of the palace with several armed soldiers.

"Search the palace for any disrupters and bring them to me at once. I'm going to the King's study room. Follow me," commanded Adak. Several soldiers followed Adak, while other soldiers dispersed quickly throughout the palace. Adak searched the palace, unaware that the three brothers were not far ahead.

"Where would Dalphon and Arisai be?" asked Poratha.

Danielle James

"I don't know? Geeee, this palace is huge and beautiful. I could get use to living in here. Look at all the beautiful colors. The ceiling is so high, it almost touches the sky," admired Aridai.

"Will you stop adoring the building and help out here," insisted Parmashta.

"They could be anywhere. I don't have a clue as to where we should began to look. You should know Parmashta. You came often to the palace with father," said Poratha.

" Yes, but unfortunately when I came I was privileged only to the guard's quarters. Let's split up and roam about the palace," suggested Parmashta.

"Noooo, I don't think that is such a good idea. If we encounter some guards we might have to fight and I think we stand a better chance together," said Poratha, "Since you fight better than the rest of us."

"Well let's not just stand here. Mordecai and Adak will be coming in here soon," said Parmashta.

"I guess any direction is better than none," said Poratha. At that moment, Adak spotted the three brothers standing in the corridor.

"Seize them!" shouted Adak.

"Ooooooops, we waited to long. Run!" bellowed Aridai. The brothers scattered when they saw the soldier's racing toward them. Adak continued his march toward the King's study. Soon he heard the clanging of swords and grunts of men fighting. He increased his pace. The soldiers followed.

The King was still locked in an intense battle with Arisai. Arisai noticed more soldiers coming down the corridor. "Seize that man!" shouted Adak. Arisai tried to fight the soldiers and the King too, but the number was too great for Arisai to withstand. He was soon overcome with force. Arisai dropped his sword and the soldiers penned him to the wall.

"Have the soldiers hold him here Adak and you follow me to the Queen's chambers. That's where Mordecai went. Hurry!" shouted the King.

176

The King, Adak and several soldiers raced toward Queen Esther's room. Swords drawn, they charged down the corridor. Minutes later, they dashed through the Queen's door. Mordecai was still engaged with Dalphon, sword to sword, fist to fist. "Adak, seize that man!" shouted the King. Adak pointed to Dalphon. The soldiers charged toward Dalphon. He tried to fight Mordecai and the soldiers too. To no avail, he was overcome with brute strength. The soldiers took his weapon and made him kneel to the floor.

"My King," cried Esther. The King moved swiftly toward Esther. She still held Obtisse in her arms upon the floor.

"My darling, are you all right? Are you hurt?" asked the King. He assisted Esther in placing Obtisse in the bed. Esther sat beside her.

"She took the sword that was meant for me," said Esther. She gazed upon Obtisse laying unconscious.

"Quickly! Adak send someone to bring the doctor," said the King. Adak motioned to one of the soldiers. He moved out quickly. Adak stared at Dalphon on the floor.

"Dalphon I told you and your brothers to leave Persia. What made you think you could overthrow the palace?" asked Adak.

"Our plan was working," said Dalphon. He thought for a moment. "You and Mordecai should not have been back at the palace so soon. You should have been gone for hours. Why did you come back so quickly?"

"Let's just say God was watching over us," said Mordecai. Dalphon spit at Mordecai's feet. The King had enough. He walked over to Dalphon.

"Raise him," demanded the King. The soldiers picked Dalphon up from the floor to face the King. The soldiers held his arm's tightly behind his back. "You are just like your father. A traitor to his King and Kingdom. Rules mean nothing to you. You think if you're clever enough to lie and cheat for what you want; that you will always get it. It seems like you would have learned from your father's mistake, instead of following behind

177

him. Bring him!" commanded the King, "We are going to find his other brothers." Everyone followed the King toward his study room where the guards held Arisai. They soon approached the King's study.

"Dalphon! I see they got you too," said Arisai. Just as they reached Arisai, the soldiers brought the other three brothers kicking and screaming down the corridor.

"There are ten of you. Where are the rest?" asked the King aggressively.

"We are in search of them," said Adak.

"This is five, where are the others?" asked the King, staring at Dalphon. Dalphon said nothing nor did his brothers.

"Where are they?" shouted the King.

"My King," said Mordecai, "His brothers are behind the massacres in the other provinces. They are being captured as we speak by Daka and the rest of our soldiers."

"How did you know that? How did you return to the palace so quickly?" asked Dalphon. "There is no way you could have known we were going to attack the palace." Dalphon paused, "Unless…" He thought, "Unless someone informed you of our plan. That's how you got back here so quickly. Right? Who was it, Mordecai?"

At that moment, Daka entered the palace, when he came down the corridor, he noticed everyone standing in the hallway. He bowed to the King upon his approach. "I have all who are responsible for the massacres in all five provinces, your Majesty. Shall I bring them in?"

"Just Haman's sons and take the rest to the dungeon. They will be sent back to their provinces to stand trial for treason. I want the citizens of each province that ignored my decree to witness what happens to traitors," said the King.

"At once your Majesty," said Daka. Daka left quickly to get Haman's sons. But Dalphon still wanted to know which brother betrayed them. He stared at Mordecai.

*"How did you know Mordecai?  Was it Aspatha?" shouted Dalphon.  Mordecai was silent.  Soon the other four brothers were brought into the corridor.*

*"There's Aridatha, Parshandatha, Valjezatha, and Aspatha." Dalphon was puzzled.  He thought.  "Where's Adalia?  Is he dead?" asked Dalphon, excitedly.  No one said a word.*

*"Someone talk to me.  Is he dead!" Dalphon shouted. Adalia heard everything from the kitchen.  He walked out into the corridor.  "No I'm not dead, I'm right here," said Adalia.*

*"What are you doing over there, when you should have been brought in with your brothers from the provinces?" shouted Dalphon.  Adalia bowed his head.  He didn't want to answer.*

*"Ohhhh, no," Dalphon shook his head, "Not you Adalia. You're the traitor?"  The soldiers still had Dalphon restrained. All the brothers were shocked.  "You're the one who betrayed your own brothers.  For what?  For what?" screamed Dalphon. "To save the neck of the people who killed your mother and father?"*

*"No, Dalphon.  It wasn't like that."  At that moment, tears began to fall from Adalia eyes.  His head was still bowed. Esther came down the corridor after hearing the shouting.*

*"Look!  Adalia!  Look!  The Queen and Mordecai are still alive.  Your parents are dead and you have just placed a noose around our necks.  For what?  For what?  Some Jews!" shouted Dalphon.  Adalia continued to cry while he stood there.  He suddenly looked up, tears streaming down his cheeks.*

*"You know, Dalphon.  We got so wrapped up in what you had told us about what father wanted us to do, that we never had a chance to think for ourselves.  It all happened so fast that we didn't even take a moment to shed tears for our mother and father.  I was so enthused about becoming a prince that mother and father didn't matter anymore.  Nothing mattered, but what I wanted.  That night at Bigota's house, after we had gone on a killing rampage, I had a chance to cry for mother and father and to think about what had just happened.  You see father told one*

179

*lie after another, after another, until the lie got so big he couldn't lie himself out of it."*

*"What are you saying?" asked Dalphon.*

*"Well first father wanted to kill Mordecai. Then it went to killing the Jews. He couldn't explain the death of the Jews after he altered the decree, so he had to kill the King to cover the lie about the Jews. Then, that led to him wanting to be King for his own personal gain. It was never about Mordecai, it was never about the Jews, and it was never about the King. It was all about what father wanted. He became so wrapped up in his own lies that he couldn't turn back. But he never thought he would get caught. That was his downfall. But he did have a back up plan and that's you Dalphon and his sons. Father trained you and he trained you well. He knew you would carry out his plan, even if the rest of us didn't want to. But, you knew how to bring out our curiosity and to get us to perform the way you wanted us to and we followed right along. Not carrying for anyone but ourselves and what we wanted."*

*"But you wanted to be wealthy and a prince too, Adalia. What happened? What changed your mind? It had to be something bizarre for you to betray your own brothers?" asked Dalphon.*

*"You're right, I did want to be a prince, until Bigota made me see what it was going to take for me to become a prince. He forced me to go on the raids, to kill the Jews. I didn't want to dirty my hands, so he made me watch. We went to the house of a Jewish family and they had a little girl. She couldn't have been more than eight or nine years old. I asked Bigota to spare her life. But he said she had to die as well, to get our point across. The prince would surely release his soldiers after hearing of the deaths of women and children. Bigota called me a coward. I guess compared to that little girl, I was. She watched as those men slayed her mother. She said not one word or muttered one groan. When she knew it was her turn, she looked me in the eyes. She still didn't let out a cry or a whimper. She only spoke a few words. She said, "God in heaven, I'm coming home." I*

*didn't understand what she said or what she meant. But from the look in her eyes, I could tell she wasn't afraid. Then Bigota without a second thought, thrust a sword into her little heart."* Tears began to flow heavier from Adalia's eyes. A quiver was in his tone of voice. *"She still didn't scream. She just fell to floor. At that moment, I thought, am I that heartless? Why did she or her mother have to die? So I could be a prince. So I could be wealthy. So I could have all the things I, I, I, wanted. Me! That little girl didn't have a clue as to why she or her mother died, but I did. I couldn't take it anymore. I knew then, what I was doing, was for all the wrong reasons."*

*"What! You turned us in for a little Jewish girl. You fool!"* shouted Dalphon.

*"Are you crazy?"* shouted Parmashta.

*"You idiot!"* screamed Arisai.

*"Father was a greedy man, filled with hatred. Nothing mattered to him but his wants and his desires. Even if it meant dragging his family down with him. All of us were turning into the same heartless individuals. Can't you see we were becoming just like him; ruthless and callous individuals toward others?"* cried Adalia.

*"Shut your mouth!"* screamed Dalphon, so enraged he broke free from the soldiers that held him. He grabbed a sword from the sheath of one of the soldiers and stuck his brother through the heart. He watched his brother fall lifeless to the floor. *"That's for me and the rest of your brothers you betrayed."* The soldiers soon seized him, stripping him of the sword. Dalphon kicked at his brother's body while the soldiers tried to drag Dalphon away. The other brothers spat at Adalia, except for Aspatha and Valjazetha. The soldiers immediately wrestled Dalphon to the floor, screaming. *"Let me go!"*

The other brothers watched in awe, while the soldiers still held them captive too. *"Hold him face down in the floor!"* shouted the King. Four soldiers held him, two held his legs and two held his arms behind his back.

181

"Do any of my other brothers feel the same way as Adalia?" asked Dalphon. He raised his head from the floor to speak. "You all vowed to avenge our parents death. Don't forget that!" None of them said a word. Aspatha and Valjazetha had tears in their eyes for their brother, Adalia and the little Jewish girl. But the King was ready to end all their lives.

"Stand him up!" shouted the King. He looked toward Esther. She had tears in her eyes as well. "My Queen, Haman's sons have dishonored the decree, they tried to take your life and the life of all the Jews as well. I place their lives in your hands. What will you have done with them?" asked the King. Esther stared at Dalphon and all Haman's sons.

"I feel that you are all victims of your father's deceitful ways. I am willing to give you all another chance at life. If you leave Persia, never to return and forgive and forget what has taken place over these past few days, then your lives will be spared. If not, the penalty is death by hanging," said Esther. Adak and Daka were shocked. They couldn't believe what the Queen had just said. Mordecai was moved emotionally at Esther's kindness and the King was surprised.

"Leave Persia. Forgive and forget! Never! My father built what we have. I'm not going to let some Jews take it away. I promised my father with my last dying breath I would keep his plan alive and revenge his death. No! You Jew. As long as I breathe or any of my brothers are alive, we will do our best to end your life."

The King was furious. He drew his sword from his sheath. The blade was high in the air, ready to strike Dalphon where he stood. "Noooo! My King," cried Esther. She moved her body in front of Dalphon. The soldiers still maintained their grip upon him.

"Esther what are you doing?" asked the King. With the look of shock and dismay upon his face. He was perplexed at her motion. He lowered his sword and placed it back into his sheath.

Esther turned to gaze into Dalphon's eyes. She only saw a blank stare. He was untouched by her reaction to save his life. She moved away from him and appealed to his brothers. "Does Dalphon speak for the rest of you too?" asked Esther.

Dalphon stared at them, while more anger and hostility mounted in his heart for the Queen.

They all shouted, "Yes!" Aspatha and Valjazetha didn't say a word, but reluctantly nodded their heads. They all agreed with Dalphon. Dalphon smiled.

Esther couldn't believe their reactions. The expressions and the actions of a couple of them indicated they wanted to live. But they followed Dalphon. She tried again.

"Don't you want to live?" she asked passionately, "You will all hang for what you have done. You can start a new life somewhere else. Some of you haven't had a chance to know what life is all about. Don't end it before you have a chance to find out. Please, don't let it end here," pleaded Esther. Dalphon grew angrier. He struggled to break free. He lunge his body forward to get at the Queen.

"Leave us be, Jewish woman. We don't want your charity. We'd rather die than serve under the likes of you or be ruled by this Jewish loving King."

"Enough!" shouted the King, "They will all hang at dawn tomorrow. Mordecai take them to the dungeon! Clear the corridors."

Mordecai motioned to Adak. "Take the prisoners to the dungeon. Get some guards to take care of the wounded."

"At once," said Adak. While all were moving about, the soldiers escorted all the brothers to the dungeon. The King walked toward Esther and embraced her. He gazed into her eyes.

"Why? Why? After stabbing Obtisse, massacring innocent people, making an attempt on your life, and stabbing his own brother, why after all that, were you willing to spare their lives? Why?" asked the King, bewildered from her actions. He released Esther and waited for her response.

183

*"My King, I don't believe those young men wanted to die. They were raised for years observing hatred, lies, and deceit. What they have become is not their fault. There is a lot of love in those young men. I can see it. It just needs to be brought out,"* said Esther.

*"Well, life as they know it will end tomorrow morning. They had their second chance. They chose to follow in their father's footsteps and so they shall."*

*"Of course, my King. I understand."* Esther gave a long sigh in remorse for the lives of those young men. *"If I may be excused?"*

*"Yes, you may go,"* said the King.

*Esther left the King to check on Obtisse.*

## Chapter 12

### Peace in the Kingdom

*The King, Adak, and Mordecai went to the King's study.*

*"Lud is still patrolling the province," said Adak.*

*"Let him stay out there the rest of this day," said Mordecai.*

*"I agree with Mordecai. Let's bring the palace and town of Shushan back to order. Clean up the streets as if this tragedy never happened. And Mordecai, be sure the gallows are prepared for the executions tomorrow. Be certain to spread the word throughout the province, that traitors will hang at dusk, for treason," said the King.*

*"It shall be done," spoke Mordecai. Mordecai and Adak bowed and left the King's study. While they walked down the corridor, Mordecai gave instructions.*

*"Adak send some men to spread the word of the executions and see that the gallows are prepared for tomorrow."*

*"At once Chief Mordecai," said Adak. He went swiftly to the guard's quarters.*

*Mordecai went to Esther's room. The door was slightly ajar. The doctor had attended to Obtisse's stab wound. He noticed Esther kneeled down beside Obtisse's bed. She still laid unconscious and Esther began to pray.*

*"Dear God in heaven please take this girl's life in Your hands and bless her. She was willing to sacrifice her life for mine. Please spare her life, so that she may share her gift of loving and sharing with others. Amen."*

*Esther stayed by her side all night long. The next morning, Esther could hear the drums roll. They were beaten loudly and slowly, for the King wanted all of Shushan at this execution. That's the only time the drums were beaten, when people were to watch. The King was among the people on this day. Mordecai rode by his side to the gallows.*

185

Danielle James

"My King, Daka has taken the prisoners of the dungeon back to their own province. I sent word that they are to be hanged as traitors before the people and that the decree will still be honored, just as you instructed," said Mordecai.

"Good!" said the King. He turned to address the crowd in the town square. "People of Shushan, I want you to know that this is what happens to traitors of the Kingdom." He pointed to the men with tightly fitted nooses around their necks at the gallows. "These men broke the law. The law that I sent forth to be honored. These men knew they were not to harm the Jews, but they not only attacked the Jews, but the Queen as well." The people were astonished. How could anyone want to harm the Queen? The news angered the people.

"They have no respect for law and order, for this, they shall be punished. Hanged! From this day forth, any citizen that refuses to obey a decree that is issued, will join these men in death. I will not tolerate disobedience of any kind. That's my final word. Let the executions take place!" shouted the King.

Mordecai raised, then lowered his hand, a motion to let the executions began. The boys were brought up to the gallows three by three, until they were no more. The crowd dispersed. The King, Mordecai and Adak were enroute to the palace when they noticed Lud riding back into town with his army of soldiers. Tired and dusty, he rode to the gallows to meet the King, Mordecai, and Adak. "My King," greeted Lud, he nodded.

"Lud, I'm glad to see you made it back. What did you encounter during your patrol of Shushan?" asked Mordecai.

"The citizens of Shushan are painfully aware of the consequences of their actions should they violate the decree. We forcefully took some citizens into custody and others died fighting our soldiers. In some areas we were too late. We counted 200 Jews and 500 Persians dead. But the battles have ended for this day as far as we could tell. The weapons I passed out earlier helped the Jews defend themselves," said Lud.

"Very good, Lud. I want you and your men to get some rest. We will still patrol the other provinces and Shushan until we are

186

absolutely certain everyone understands that the King is serious about his decree being honored. Take your men back to the palace, eat well and rest," said Mordecai.

Lud did as Mordecai instructed. The King was listening to the conversation between Mordecai and Lud. The King rode closer to Mordecai.

"Mordecai do you think it necessary to patrol the provinces for·a few more days after what the people have just witnessed here?" asked the King.

"My King, some people have no fear of authority or the law, especially if they believe they won't get caught. The soldiers will be given orders to slay anyone that does not respect the decree. I will ensure that the decree is honored, your Highness," stated Mordecai firmly.

The King, Adak, and Mordecai went back to the palace. Upon their arrival, Mordecai and Adak immediately sent messengers to all the provinces to let them know the King's decree was still in effect. As the days passed, all fighting finally subsided. And in every province and in every city, the King's decree was honored. The Jews were no longer crying and mourning in the streets. Mordecai went to see the King and Queen in the throne room. He knocked.

"Enter," said the King. Mordecai bowed when he entered the room.

"My King and Queen, I believe the fighting has ended. I have heard nothing of fighting for the last three days from any of the provinces."

"Excellent! Then it is safe to say that Shushan and the rest of my kingdom are back to normal."

"I would say that, my King," said Mordecai with a smile.

"I feel you should be honored Mordecai. Your relentless efforts have proven to save a lot of lives that could have been lost," said the King.

"I feel you should be honored too, Chief Mordecai," added Esther, smiling.

"I thank you my King and Queen, but I was just doing my job."

"You shall be honored Mordecai," insisted the King, "And this time I will not take no for an answer."

"Then, my soldiers will ride with me. I couldn't have done it without their support," said Mordecai.

"As you wish. Tomorrow you will take several of your soldiers in a King's royal dress wear and ride among the town square. Let the people know it was you and your men that prevented a lot of bloodshed. I will have Ischdi write a decree and post it before the day ends," said the King.

"This time, Uncle, you shall be honored." Mordecai bowed and started to leave the throne room.

"Ohhhh, Uncle, one question before you leave."

"Yes, my Queen."

"Where did you learn to fight so well? I was fearful that Dalphon would have the upper hand."

"Hazor, my Queen. He trained me well in the days of our friendship." Mordecai appeared sad when he spoke Hazor's name.

Mordecai bowed and left the throne room. He patrolled Shushan for the rest of the day.

When night grew near, Mordecai laid down to rest that evening. He looked toward heaven and began to pray.

"Dear God in heaven, thank You for the lives we saved. Thank You for the strength and the wisdom to fight those battles. I could not have succeeded without You watching over me. My Father in heaven, I want to thank You for all that You have done for Esther and myself. We have come a long way from burlap clothing and a one-room rectangle house. Thank You for all the blessings we have received. Without Your loving kindness, nothing we wanted to achieve would have been possible. Thank You Lord. My faith will always be in You. Amen."

Mordecai laid down to rest another night. As the new dawn came for another bright and glorious morning, Mordecai readied himself for his day of honor. He was dressed in royal apparel. Mordecai had on a solid blue cape with white trim around his neck. The garment he wore was made of fine dark purple linen. A great crown of gold sat upon his head. He rode throughout the province of Shushan on the King's finest horse with his army of soldiers behind him. The City of Shushan was glad and rejoiced.

The King and Queen watched from their palace balcony with Obtisse at their side. The crowd honored Mordecai and the soldiers with cheers and flowers thrown at the feet of their horses as they rode by.

"My King," said Esther, "May we declare this day a holiday and that on this day all shall rejoice, sing and be glad."

The King reached for Esther's hand and lovingly placed a kiss on her cheek. Esther smiled.

"So let it be said. So let it be done," said the King.

And so it was written in the book of the land, that the day be declared a holiday. And it was told that Mordecai had the King's honor and respect. And his name was great among the Jews. From that day forth Esther and Mordecai sought wealth for the people to bring them from poverty and they spoke of peace and love across the land.

# About the Author

Raised near pecan groves and cotton fields in a small town called Rayville in the state of Louisiana, she lived with four brothers and sisters. Her father was a sole parent when her mother died at the tender age of thirty-nine. She watched her father work in the cotton gin all day, while her older brothers and sisters picked cotton on the days of no school. Staring at the rough and skin torn hands of her family from picking cotton, she decided this was not the life she wanted to lead. Perhaps the military would bring a better way of life, especially from all the commercials of "Be All You Can Be, Join the Army" and travel the world.

This sounded great, after five years in the military and making the rank of Captain, the choice of staying in or getting out became clear. After many months of camping in the wilderness with all types of bugs, hot days, cold nights, no bathrooms, no running water, eating meals from a plastic package, and sleeping without a night light; she chose to get out. After leaving the Army, there had to be a better way to see the world. She joined the Navy. Not as a naval officer or an enlisted person, but as a civilian. The opportunity to see the world wasn't as great, but there weren't any bugs around either.

Printed in the United States
2519